# ALMOST HITCHED

KYLIE GILMORE

Cover design by Sweet 'N Spicy Designs

Published by: Extra Fancy Books

ISBN-13: 978-1-942238-21-8

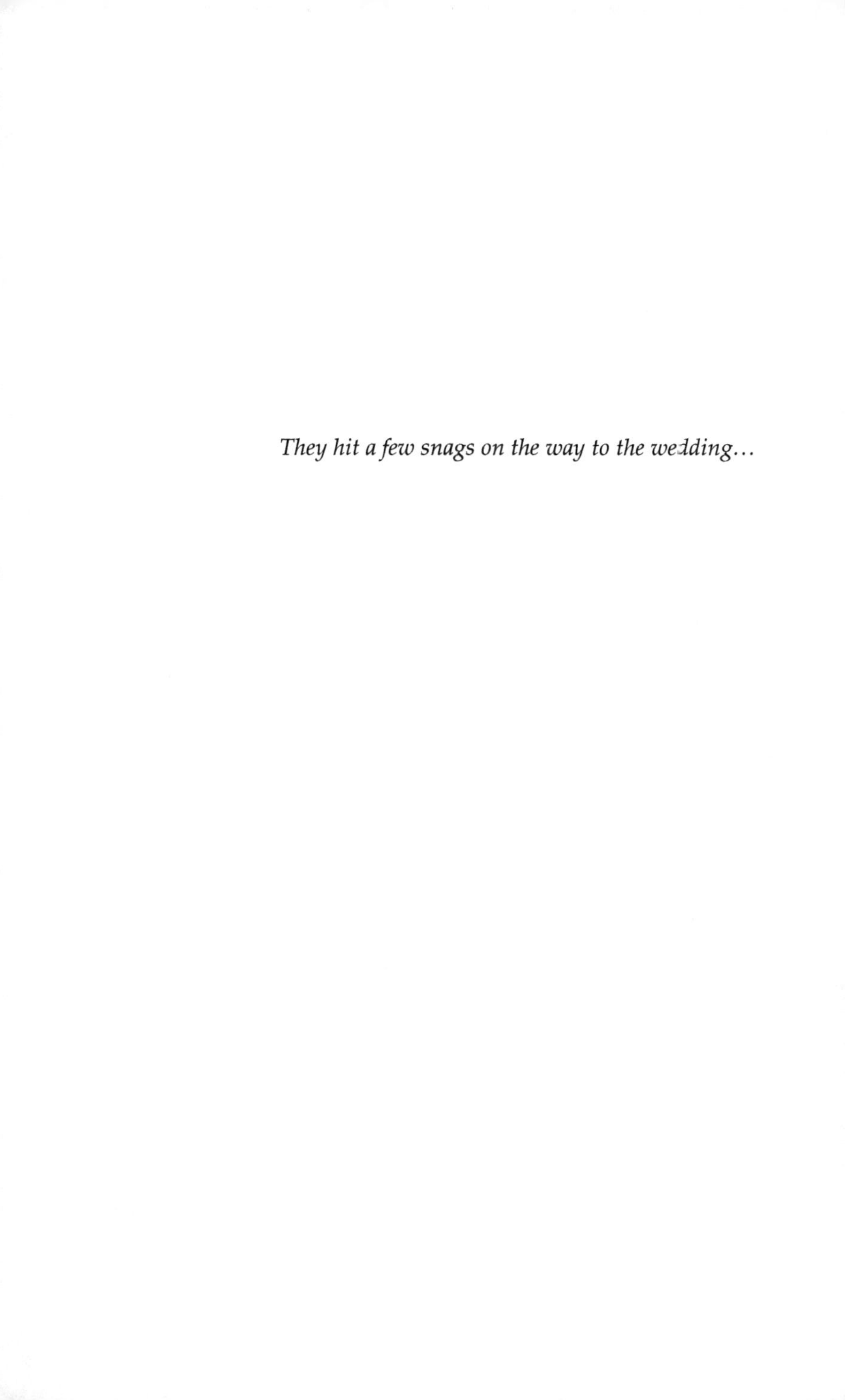
They hit a few snags on the way to the wedding...

**1**

---

*Aw, yeah. Life is good.* Ian Furnukle stepped out of his favorite neighborhood Boston bar late Friday night and headed back to his apartment with a bounce in his step. Everything in his life was *finally* coming together. He had a beautiful sexy girl-friend (long distance for now) and a new job opportunity that would give him and Kate a chance to be together in the same location. He and Kate Lewis had a history that spanned nearly five years, three states, and several detours into different relationships. They were friends first, off and on lovers, and permanently tied by family ever since his older brother Barry married Kate's older sister, Amber. He'd been Kate's first five years ago, *aw, yeah,* and he hoped to be her last. They'd committed to a long-distance relationship over the previous Christmas break. Now he had an opportunity that would give him roots in Boston.

Looking to the future, a year from now when Kate finished her postdoc fellowship at the University of Chicago's particle physics laboratory, he hoped to convince her to find a tenure-track professor job in one of the many Boston-area universities.

It would mark the start of their life together.

Only seven more days until he could see his beautiful sexy girlfriend in person. He'd be flying out to Chicago for Kate's spring break. It had been nearly three months since he'd last seen her in person, and they had a lot of sexy times to make up for. Though Kate had become quite adept at the Skype sex. Tonight was a Skype night. *Aw, yeah, baby, touch yourself. That's right. You're making me so hot.* (Cue moans and gasps. Hers.)

He smiled to himself. That was one of the things he loved about Kate. She was direct, open, and honest about everything, including sex. He never had to wonder what she wanted or if she liked something. She flat out told him. The inner workings of the female mind had never been so clear.

He reached his brownstone apartment, unlocked the door, and pushed it open.

"Surprise!"

He jumped, his heart pounding against his rib cage. "Kate! What're you doing here?" She wore a pink satin robe. Her blond hair was out of its usual half bun and fell in soft waves over her shoulders. Her legs were bare, so were her feet. Was she naked under that robe?

"I'm surprising you because I wanted to do something you really liked." Her eyebrows scrunched together. "You did give me a key to your place. Did I get it wrong? Do you not like surprises? You surprise me so much I thought for sure…" She trailed off and wrung her hands together.

He pulled her hands apart and gave her a big hug. Her head settled against his chest. "You got it right. I love surprises." He tipped her chin up and kissed her, but before he could take things deeper, she pulled away.

She held up a palm, her blue eyes sparkling behind large tortoiseshell glasses. Then she stared at his forehead. "You cut your hair. It's not in your eyes anymore."

He'd gotten a close-cropped cut to look more professional for his job interview, but he didn't want to talk about that right now. He wanted to rip that robe off her. "Yeah, I got a haircut. Take off your robe."

She gave him an impish smile. "There's more surprise."

"More surprise than you showing up here the week before I was supposed to show up there?"

"Yes."

"Wait, I thought your spring break was next week."

"I lied in order to create the element of surprise."

"But I'm visiting you next week."

"I have an easy week and will have plenty of time for you."

He kicked off his shoes. "Okay, I'm ready for more surprise. Are you naked under that robe?"

She untied the belt of the robe, but kept it closed. "Do you recognize this robe?"

He studied it for a moment. "That's the robe you wore the first time we were together."

She flashed a quick smile. "Precisely. For the deflowering." His lips twitched on her term for losing her virginity. "And do you remember what I told you after?"

He pressed his lips together, serious now. He remembered all right. Damn near killed him. "You said you couldn't be hydrogen." He'd been really into her after he took her virginity (as she demanded), but she'd informed him she was only twenty-one and couldn't be hydrogen. Translation: only one electron (guy) orbiting her. She wanted to sow her wild oats in grad school, never having dated before him. He'd been twenty-four and experienced enough to know when great sex meant something more. But she'd made him wait.

"Correct!" she exclaimed and flung open the robe.

Totally worth the wait.

She wasn't naked. Still, the effect was stunning—white fuzzy suspenders with a white fuzzy strip of fabric across her breasts, nipple height. So much skin. She shrugged off the robe and tossed it back toward the sofa. His gaze trailed lower to what the suspenders were attached to—white bikini panties topped by a fuzzy waistband that matched the suspenders.

He reached for her, and she twirled away, laughing. "I still have more surprise!"

"That wasn't it? Because this is great."

She beamed, and his breath caught. Kate hardly ever smiled that big, she saved it for truly joyous occasions, and the effect made her even more beautiful.

"Nope!" she exclaimed. "Bigger."

He cocked his head. "Can I see the back of this outfit?"

She turned, giving him a view of bare beautiful back and sweet curvy ass. She smiled at him over her shoulder. "Do you like it? There's hidden double-sided tape on my breasts to hold it in place. You'll have to peel it off slowly."

He groaned. "Get over here."

She turned to face him and took a step back. "No touching, kissing, or groping until I give you the rest of the surprise."

"You'd better hurry up," he growled.

She giggled, which warmed his heart. She so rarely giggled. She was a very serious physicist. He loved that he could bring out this lighter side of her.

"Ian! I can't think when you touch me. You know there's a short circuit from my brain to my libido!"

"I love your short circuit."

She tossed her hair over her shoulder. "I blame it on chemistry."

"Uh-huh. Give it to me."

She slowly ran her hands down the suspenders from her shoulders, over her breasts, to her narrow waist. He couldn't take his eyes off those hands. He'd watched her touch herself for weeks at his direction over Skype, but in person it was torture. He wanted his hands on her so badly. Her hands crossed the bar that went between her breasts, and she let out a soft moan as she stroked across her nipples. His cock pulsed with need. Her hands met in the middle of the bar before sliding back to her sides. "You watched the shape of my outfit," she said, her voice a husky purr that showed her own arousal. "You recognize it?"

He blinked, his mind fuzzy as primal caveman instinct took over. *Me no want surprise. Me want woman.* "Just tell me. I can't think."

She giggled, and his eyes snapped to hers. "The outfit is an H. I'm hydrogen." She closed the distance between them, hips swaying, a small smile playing over her sweet pink lips. "And you're the one electron orbiting me."

Yes, he knew all this. They were monogamous. It was why she'd gone on the pill.

"I love you in this," he told her.

"I had it made special for you," she said in a husky voice before dropping to her knees in front of him. *Aw, yeah.* His favorite. What little blood supply he had left in his brain deserted him. He was about to bust the zipper on his jeans.

"Marry me," she said.

*What!*

He cleared his throat, suddenly light-headed. "Huh?"

She was still on her knees, gazing up at him adoringly. "I said marry me."

"Yes," he heard himself say as if from some great distance.

"Oh, Ian!" She stood and hugged him. He wrapped his arms around her, speechless. Yes, he'd hoped to marry her. One day, down the road. Maybe after another year of long-distance dating. Not quite yet. Marriage was serious business —mortgage, bills, kids, the works. Heavy, heavy responsibilities.

She went up on tiptoe and kissed him. "I love you." The words that used to be so difficult for her flowed freely. That was a gift he knew he could never throw away.

"I love you too," he said, his voice husky with emotion. He slid her glasses off, setting them on the foyer table.

"You know I can only see things close up without my glasses," she said in a teasing voice.

He scooped her up and tossed her over his shoulder. "This close enough for you?"

She giggled madly. "I have a very good view of your pants pocket." She patted his butt, and he palmed her ass. She moaned. Yup. This was happening.

He took her to his bedroom, set her gently on the bed, stripped quickly and joined her. He peeled her carefully out of the hydrogen costume. God, she was beautiful. He kissed and tasted every inch of exposed skin.

"Oh, Ian! This is the first time we'll make love as an engaged couple."

He pulled back for a moment, still in shock that somehow

he'd gotten engaged, but then she pushed him to his back, climbed on board, and sank down onto him. He hissed out a breath and grabbed her by the hips, guiding her to his rhythm. His intense need far outweighed any worries about the future. She threw her head back, her hands running through her hair, making him crazed with lust. It had been too long. He sat up, bringing her close for the angle that stroked her *yes*-spot as he thrust. He knew the moment he hit the target.

"Yes! Yes! Yes!" she hollered, her nails digging into his shoulders. And then she quieted, her breath coming in quick gasps, which meant she was close.

"Now," he rasped in her ear. "Come for me."

And she did, shuddering around him, milking him with her release, and he let go with a long low groan. He held her close, catching his breath, and then kissed her tenderly. She smiled against his mouth. He settled them into bed a few moments later, spooning her from behind, and fell into a deep, satisfied sleep.

He woke at three a.m. in a cold sweat.

## 2

_______

Kate heard a weird whimpering noise coming from Ian's side of the bed in the middle of the night. He was on his back, and she hovered over him. "Are you okay?" she whispered.

He jerked. "Huh? What's happening?"

She stroked his hair and realized he was sweating. "Are you sick? I remember what to do." Last Christmas Ian had gotten food poisoning from a turkey she'd undercooked and ended up in the hospital with severe dehydration. He'd since provided her with instructions spelling out exactly how to take care of someone who was sick, which had been most helpful. You were supposed to touch the patient and say loving things as you waited on them hand and foot. He was especially adamant about the foot part, demanding regular foot massages.

He blew out a breath. "No. Just a bad dream." He pushed the blanket down to his waist, probably to cool off, but she couldn't help gazing at his beautiful naked body for a long moment in the dim glow of a nearby streetlight.

She stroked his warm skin from his shoulder down to his bicep, reveling in the feel of hard muscle. Ian was extremely sexy—tall and broad shouldered with defined muscles in his arms, pecs, and abs, even his back was delicious with sleek muscle. He also had a dark stubbled jaw that scraped against her wherever he kissed her, bringing shivers of pleasure, and a deep rumbly voice that made her insides flutter. All the markings of hot masculinity with the bonus of warm loving brown eyes, an easygoing temperament that relaxed her, and a sharp mind that understood all her quirks—her tendency to think of everything in terms of science, her compulsive equation writing, even her formal Spock-like tone when emotions overwhelmed her. Ian understood and accepted her like no one ever had before. Of course, she had to propose.

Besides, she was twenty-five years old (to his twenty-eight), which meant the timing was finally right for a commitment. Unlike the first time they got together when she was only twenty-one. She stroked his chest over the rough hair that formed an inverted triangle leading to a satisfyingly thick —she stopped her dirty thoughts. He'd just had a bad dream. He needed to think of super happy things like their engagement. "We should call Barry and Amber to tell them the good news." Their married siblings (her sister, his brother) had been so happy when she and Ian officially became a couple nearly three months ago.

He rolled to his side, facing her. "Later," he mumbled before closing his eyes.

She lay on her side too, excited all over again about being engaged. She'd never been engaged before. "Of course. I'm not going to call at…" She squinted over at the digital alarm clock on his nightstand. "Three oh three a.m. I'll wait until seven. Violet will be up by then, waking everyone." Violet was her and Ian's brilliant adorable niece. She was turning two on Monday and tomorrow she and Ian would go to her birthday party in Clover Park, Connecticut.

She ran her fingers through his light brown hair; the shorter cut felt rougher and made the angles of his face even more manly. She sighed a happy sigh, thinking about how excited her older sister, Amber, would be when Kate shared her wonderful news. Amber was Kate's best friend—her only female friend too—and would probably want to throw them an engagement party. Definitely want to go wedding gown shopping together. Maybe she'd even forgo a veil in favor of a tiara. Kate didn't have a lot of girly frilly things as a kid, her mom didn't want her to feel restricted by gender stereotypes, but Kate longed for them. Ian encouraged her to wear dresses and silly fun things like tutus. He'd gotten her a purple tutu as a New Year's gift.

"Maybe you could go wedding gown shopping with me and Amber," she said.

He groaned.

"You're so good at picking out stuff I like. Remember you said you'd get me a tiara to go with my tutu."

No response.

She stroked his hair some more, enjoying the contrast of soft hair and rough cut. "Of course, I'll be getting you an engagement ring. I didn't know your size, but I'll tell you right now it will be onyx. Very manly and solid. You don't have to get me a ring since I was the one to ask you to marry me. Anyway, I never wear jewelry."

"Kate," he growled, causing a flutter low in her belly.

She threw an arm and leg over him. "Yes, fiancé?"

"Do we have to talk about this right now?"

That seemed like a hint. Clearly he was too tired to discuss his future ring. They should probably shop for it in person at a store so he could try on different options. She took the hint, appreciating the way Ian always came through with clear messages that she could understand, unlike most people who left her confused with their subtext and tones meant to convey who knew what. She didn't even try to guess anymore because she was nearly always wrong.

She stroked his bicep again. She'd so missed him over the last couple of months. Then she remembered he was waiting for an answer on the necessity of discussing the ring right now. "Of course not," she assured him. He remained quiet, eyes closed.

A beat passed while Kate wondered where they should get married and when. Sooner would be better than later. Maybe in May after her postdoc fellowship was completed. But who would plan it? She worked long hours, and Ian traveled a lot for his job as a consultant on computer applications.

He had a PhD in computer science. Hmm…her sister had her hands full with her painting career and Violet, so she probably couldn't plan a wedding either.

"We should hire a wedding planner," she told him.

No response.

"Of course, we'll need to set a date before that."

Silence.

"And possibly a venue. I think Chicago might be too hard for most of our fam—" Her wedding planning was cut off when Ian's large hand wrapped around the back of her neck, pulled her close, and his lips met hers in a hard demanding kiss. His tongue delved into her mouth. Her last thought before her brain shut down was that they were both naked and that was good, though she suspected he'd tripped the circuit from her brain to her libido just to shut her up.

She let him.

For a really long time.

She waited until they'd both been thoroughly satisfied and lay panting in the aftermath before returning to the topic at hand.

"I'm keeping my name," she informed him once she could speak. "I've already racked up several publication credits under the Kate Lewis name."

He tucked her head against his chest. "Shh…"

"But our children can be Lewis-Furnukle to avoid confusion. Like Barry and Amber did with Violet."

He tilted her chin up and pressed his mouth to hers. Her brain shut down again. Then he stayed like that, not moving at all, just covering her mouth.

She pulled away. "You were just trying to quiet me with your sexy stuff, weren't you?"

He cupped the back of her head and pulled her close, covering her mouth with his own again. She closed her eyes, suddenly tired. His hand dropped from her head as he eased back and let out a soft snore. She relaxed even more. They'd have plenty of time for wedding planning in the morning.

Only the next morning, when she sat up and reached for her cell phone to call Amber, Ian tackled her, drawing her down under him, making her pant and shake and tremble until she couldn't think of anything but his name. Sneaky wild fiancé.

Ian took a shower later that morning, debating if he should admit he had cold feet. He never, ever wanted to hurt Kate, so he thought maybe he shouldn't. It would probably pass. He'd just been surprised, that was all. Soon his brain would catch up with his new reality, and he'd think this was all great news.

On the other hand, every time Kate mentioned the engagement and wedding planning, a raw primal fear clawed at him. Like he was trapped. He channeled that trapped animal feeling into a roaring, escaped animal by taking her again and again. But that wasn't practical long-term. After their two weeks together—this week in Boston, next week in Chicago—they'd be long distance again. A little too much time apart would really snowball the wedding planning stuff.

He stepped out of the shower, and Kate appeared in her pink robe and handed him a towel. "Guess what?" she asked.

He snagged the towel and gave her a quick kiss. "What?"

"Barry and Amber want to take us out to a congratulations dinner!"

He swallowed. "Oh. You called them already?"

"Yes! Just now. They're so happy for us. Barry wants you to call as soon as you're dressed."

He dried off. "Okay, great."

"It is great. Amber said we should stay the weekend at their place. We'll go out to dinner tonight after Violet's birthday party, and tomorrow we can shop for wedding gowns! I've already staked out three bridal boutiques near Clover Park. I'd love for you to come!"

"And I'd love for *you* to come," he growled, palming her ass and pulling her up against him. He kissed her long and deep. She rubbed herself against him, and he thrust his leg between hers. He knew sexing her up was a cop-out. He didn't care. He needed more time. The last thing he wanted was for Kate to know about the cold feet problem when she was this excited about their engagement. This trapped feeling would pass.

It had to. His brother would call him on it the minute he saw him.

He slid a hand into her hair and kissed her roughly. She moaned against his mouth and everything else faded away.

**3**

———

Ian rang the bell at his older brother's house in Clover Park, a white colonial with green shutters, and took a deep breath. Kate was literally bouncing with excitement at his side. The door swung open.

"There she is," Barry sang, his arms out to Kate, "the newest Lewis-Furnukle!"

Kate beamed and stepped inside. Barry gave her a big bear hug. His oldest brother by seven years looked like an older version of Ian—six foot, lean, light brown hair, and brown eyes. Kate always said Ian was a cuter, younger version of Barry. She was biased, but Ian let her keep thinking that.

"Congratulations!" Barry said, taking them both in.

"Thank you!" Kate exclaimed.

"Thanks," Ian mumbled.

Barry turned to Ian. "So how'd you do it? Rose petals and candles? Romantic dinner?"

Ian rubbed the back of his neck. They hadn't gotten their story straight. *Kate wore a skimpy hydrogen costume and went on her knees, making me think with my little head* didn't sound all that romantic.

Kate looked to him, and he shook his head, silently telling her he had no clue what to say.

Honest as always, Kate announced, "I proposed to Ian in a hydrogen costume I had made especially for the occasion."

Barry blinked. "Well, uh…"

Amber and Violet appeared. "Of course she did," Amber said with a smile, her blue eyes sparkling with amusement. Like Kate, Amber was petite and blonde, though the artsy Amber sported violet streaks in her hair. Violet's blond hair was in pigtails, her eyes brown like her dad. Her hair would likely darken. He and his two older brothers had all been blond when they were little.

Kate rushed to hug her sister, saying, "I love you." Then she scooped up Violet in a big hug. "I love you!"

"Wuv you, Tate," Violet said. She had trouble with her Ls and Ks. Her Ss were lispy too. So adorable.

Amber hugged Ian and whispered in his ear, "You're good for her. Look at her with all the hugs and I love yous."

He looked over where Kate was now smiling and rubbing noses with Violet. His heart squeezed. She adored their niece. There was a time when he thought Kate was too cold to adore anything but physics.

"That's just the Violet effect," he said under his breath.

Amber kept an arm around him. "It's you, being in love. She has friends now at the university."

He didn't know that. "That's great." Though it occurred to him that they must be guy friends because she was the only female in the particle physics laboratory, and maybe that was why she hadn't mentioned it.

Barry gave him a hug and pounded him on the back. "I knew you two would get engaged one day. A little sooner than I thought, but who cares? It was inevitable."

"What evable?" Violet asked.

Kate set her down, and Violet ran to Ian, grabbing him around the legs and making his knees buckle. He snagged her by the waist and flipped her upside down. "How's my favorite niece?"

Violet giggled. "Good! I ate a hot dog." Ian set her down to prevent the hot dog from coming back up. "More nieces?"

She peeked around his legs like he might be hiding a few. "Where?"

Ian tapped her nose. "Just you."

"Oh." She was sharp. She knew favorite meant a preferred choice among many. Violet turned her attention back to Kate. "What evable?"

"In-ev-i-ta-ble," Kate enunciated clearly, "is something that's definitely going to happen."

"Wite tate!" Violet exclaimed.

"Like cake," Amber translated.

Kate beamed. "That's right!"

Violet ran into the living room and grabbed a small pink backpack off the sofa. She sat on the floor with it.

"That's her stash of toys," Amber said. "We put away the rest for the party. So tell us everything wedding! When, where, details!"

"Still plenty of time for all that planning stuff," Ian said. "How can we help get ready for the party?"

Amber and Barry exchanged a look. Amber immediately guided Kate over to the sofa.

Barry narrowed his eyes at Ian. *Caught!* He knew Barry would call him on this cold feet business. "Help me get some drinks for the ladies."

Ian swallowed hard. "Sure." He turned to Amber and Kate. "What can I get you?"

"Bring us all some ice water," Amber said. "And bring Violet a juice box."

Violet leaped up. "Juice!"

"Stay with Mommy," Barry ordered.

Once they were in the kitchen, Ian watched his brother get out the glasses. The silence stretched as Barry pulled out the ice tray and cracked it, tossed ice in the glasses, and poured the water.

Finally Ian couldn't take the silent judgment anymore. "She surprised me!" he whispered fiercely.

Barry lined up the glasses on the counter before turning to him and asking quietly, "So you don't want to be engaged?"

Ian lifted one shoulder up and down. "I'm getting used to it."

Barry crossed his arms and leaned against the counter. "It's a little fast. You've only been dating three months." Barry kept his voice low, out of consideration for Kate probably, but Violet was chattering so loudly Ian didn't think they'd hear anything from this distance anyway.

Ian rubbed the back of his neck. "Not even three months. Almost three months."

"It's too much too soon."

Ian blew out a breath, relieved his older brother seemed to understand the prickly situation. "Yeah."

"She's new at relationships," Barry said.

Ian stifled a groan. "I know." Barry had a soft spot for Kate, who had idolized Barry from the moment they met for his achievements with his groundbreaking app. Kate had a keen appreciation for intellectual breakthroughs. In any case, Ian was well aware he was only Kate's second relationship. He'd kept tabs on her over the years. He also knew her first relationship had lasted two months. Maybe she thought that their relationship passing the two-month mark meant it was time. Hell, he'd been with his ex for three years and never even considered proposing.

Somehow things had gotten really serious really fast with Kate. He forced a slow deep breath.

Barry cocked a brow, probably waiting for Ian to say something reassuring about not hurting Kate, but he feared he was going to end up doing exactly that. If everyone could just stop talking about the wedding, he might be able to deal.

He grabbed two glasses of ice water, prepared to make his escape. Barry fetched the juice box, tucked it under his elbow, and grabbed the other two glasses.

Ian had only taken one step toward freedom when Barry stopped him.

"Ian, wait."

He turned. "What?"

Barry's brown eyes were kind and completely nonjudgmental. "You can tell her you're not ready. Honesty is important in a relationship."

Ian stepped closer to his brother and lowered his voice. "And break her heart? Did you see how happy she is?"

Barry inclined his head.

"I'll get there. I told you she surprised me."

"Okay then," Barry agreed easily. "Leave that to you."

"Thank you." He turned, thinking he'd finally put an end to the painful conversation when his brother quietly spoke again.

"It's better to hurt her a little with the truth now than wait until you're in deeper down the road."

Ian kept walking. He needed time. That was all.

When he returned to the living room, Kate and Amber were looking at an iPad, chatting about necklines and lace. Apparently, they were already shopping for a wedding gown. His gut churned. He set the glasses on the coffee table and took a seat on the floor next to Violet, who plunked a mermaid doll in his lap.

Kate sent him a questioning look. He looked away, not having an easy answer. He wouldn't be able to sex her up here as a distraction. It was time for the Serious Talk.

Kate was getting a very weird feeling. Something was off with Ian. He looked way too serious for a man holding a mermaid doll. She'd ask him tonight when they were alone in the guest room. And this time she would make sure he didn't touch her. No short-circuiting this important of a conversation. She focused her attention back on Amber. Her sister was seven years older, similar in looks, but with a much more outgoing artistic personality due to her having a different mother than Kate. Amber's mom was a famous artist living in Paris. Kate's mom was a physicist at Princeton University. So was her and Amber's dad. Amber was a bit of an oddball in their family, not being a physicist.

Amber exited the wedding gown website and set the iPad

down. "Bad luck for the groom to see," she said to Kate. "So," she said brightly, taking both Kate and Ian in, "have you set a date?"

Kate looked to Ian, who seemed to be avoiding her eyes. "Not yet," Kate said. "Maybe next May or June after I wrap up my postdoc. Or earlier if the fellowship opportunity in Geneva works out. They have special benefits for spouses."

Ian's head snapped up. "Geneva?"

She nodded. "At the Large Hadron Collider in Switzerland. It's the largest most powerful particle accelerator in the world. The director of our program wants me to apply for a fellowship. If I get it, I'll spend the last year of my postdoc there. It's an extraordinary opportunity. That's why I have an easy week next week. I'll be filling out the paperwork for my application."

"Wow!" Barry said.

"Wow!" Violet echoed.

"That's awesome!" Amber exclaimed. "I remember you mentioned you wanted to run some experiments at the Hadron collider."

Barry sent Amber an approving look. Her sister did her best to keep up with Kate's physics career though she understood very little about it. Barry understood more. He was a brilliant software engineer that had developed an app, Giggle Snap, that used a groundbreaking compression algorithm to share sound files across social networks. It made him big-time money. Now he ran a fro-yo shop for fun and developed apps on the side.

Ian took a long drink of ice water. Kate couldn't quite put her finger on the problem, but Ian seemed tense.

"You should get married here," Amber said. "Then I can help you plan it. Do you remember where me and Bare got married at the big mansion in Clover Park?"

Kate focused on her sister, who was, as usual, relaxed and cheerful. "Yes. It was beautiful."

"The official name is Ludbury House," Amber said. "Anyway, they have a wedding planner now. Maybe we could meet with her while you're in town. She often takes appointments on Sundays."

"What do you think?" Kate asked Ian.

"Whatever you want," Ian mumbled.

That wasn't like Ian either. He was usually very decisive. Her brows scrunched together as she puzzled over Ian's strange behavior.

"Guys don't enjoy wedding planning as much as we do," Amber said in a soothing voice. "I planned our wedding with Susan." That was Barry and Ian's mom. "Except for the music. That was all Bare."

Kate nodded. Amber was probably right. She understood a lot more about interpersonal relationships than Kate did. That would definitely explain Ian's weirdness when Kate talked about wedding planning. For a moment there, she worried that he didn't want to get married. She reassured herself that he wouldn't have said yes to her proposal if he didn't want to. She would never agree if she didn't want to do something. Ian probably just wanted to show up in a tux. She, on the other hand, was imagining the Cinderella experience like she'd never had before. A horse-drawn carriage. A beautiful white poufy gown, a tiara, shiny crystal and silver slippers—the works. White flowers, pink flowers, red flowers. Doves. Confetti. Bubbles. Violet would be the flower girl. Kate could already picture herself and Ian joyfully running down the aisle as husband and wife to applause with bubbles, confetti, rice, and doves releasing into the sky.

"Have you told Dad and Maxine?" Amber asked, popping Kate's fantasy bubble. Maxine was her mom, Amber's stepmom. Just the mention of her mom's name was sobering. Her mom was humorless, all of her focus on her physics work. Kate had been uncomfortably similar before she fell in love with Ian. Love was a powerful phenomenon, making her relaxed and happy in body and mind. She was grateful she finally got to experience it.

"No, I didn't tell them yet," Kate said.

Ian stood abruptly. "I'm going to grab our bags from the car." He left.

She bit her lip, more than a little worried about Ian's odd behavior.

Amber snagged her cell. "Better to give them a heads-up. You know Maxine doesn't do surprises well."

Neither did Kate until Ian gave her a few really fun surprises. Now she was more open to them, though still a little slow in reacting appropriately to what was usually a positive thing.

Kate sighed. "They're not going to be excited."

"They'll be happy for you," Amber said, already tapping her phone. "Trust me." Kate heard the phone ring and Amber shoved the phone at her as soon as her mom answered.

"Hi, Mom."

"Hello, Kate. Why are you calling from Amber's phone? Are you visiting her?"

"Yes, I flew to Boston to surprise Ian, and we drove to Barry and Amber's for Violet's party."

"We're on our way and should arrive in two hours, barring traffic." Her parents were very precise and scheduled. They liked to arrive exactly fifteen minutes after a party's start time and planned accordingly for their drive from Princeton, New Jersey. "Why did you call if we're going to see you in person?"

"I wanted to tell you the good news." She sucked in a breath, sure her mom was going to rain on her happy parade. "Ian and I are getting married."

"Oh, I see. And when will this occur?"

"I don't know yet."

The phone went silent, there was a rustle, and then her dad got on. "Hello, Kate. Your mom just told me the news. He's a nice young man."

"Yes."

"Okay, then. We'll see you in two hours, barring traffic."

"Okay," Kate said. The phone went dead. "Bye."

Amber pasted a smile on. "See? Happy for you in their weird way."

"I guess."

Amber patted her shoulder. "By the time they get here, it'll have sunk in and they'll be ready with congratulations."

"Woo-hoo," she said, twirling her finger in the air in a big show of fake cheer.

Amber laughed and grabbed her arm. "Look at you with the sarcasm! I'll corrupt you yet!"

Kate laughed.

"I'm already corrupting her," Ian said, returning to the living room with her wheeled suitcase and his duffel bag. "This one is queen of the Skype."

Kate's cheeks burned. "Ian! Our weekly phone sex is private!"

Ian winked. "I didn't say phone sex. You did."

"Hey, hey, hey," Barry said, gesturing to Violet. "Little ears."

Violet sipped her juice, oblivious.

"Awww," Amber said. "I'm so happy for you guys. I remember our engagement was such a fun, exciting time."

Ian grunted and headed upstairs with their bags.

Kate wrung her hands together, positive something was off with Ian because, so far, the only fun, exciting engagement time she'd had was with her sister.

4

Kate spent the next hour helping Amber while Barry and Ian played with Violet in the backyard. She was secretly relieved for a little space from Ian. He was so tense and weird, it was really weighing on her. They needed to talk privately. For now, she kept busy wrapping presents, getting favor bags ready, and preparing food for the party. Amber had invited their parents, Barry and Ian's mom, and six children from Violet's mommy and me playgroup.

"You and Ian want kids?" Amber asked as they pulled a plastic pink tablecloth over a small kids table.

"Definitely," Kate said, though they hadn't talked about it. They both adored Violet, so she figured they wanted the same thing. "The sooner the better. I'm twenty-five, so I'd like to have them while my eggs are still viable."

"Uh-huh," Amber said. "Talk to me again after the party."

Two hours later, Kate was in shock. The children were maniacs. Violet alone always seemed so sweet and reasonable. Seven two-year-olds together fed off each other in a frenzy of energy. Barry came out in his Dancing Cow costume from his fro-yo shop, and they went nuts with earsplitting shrieks. Bubbles made them wild and run into each other, wailing as heads collided. And, worst of all, after eating chocolate cake and ice cream, they made the living room furniture their playground, climbing and jumping on every-thing. Amber and Barry herded them outside, and the chil-dren ran in circles in the backyard, screaming at the top of their lungs for no good reason.

Ian appeared at her side and wrapped an arm around her shoulders.

She sagged heavily against him. "No rush for kids."

"Nope."

Ian's mom, Susan, joined them. She was a friendly, affec-tionate woman with short light brown hair and bright brown eyes. Basically the mom Kate wished she had. She brightened. Maybe now that she was marrying Ian, she would get a second chance at the warm and friendly mom thing.

Susan hugged them both and then beamed. "Finally get a minute alone with you two! Congratulations! My boys sure have good taste!"

"Thank you," Kate said.

Susan smiled warmly at Kate. "Anything I can do to help with wedding planning, just say the word. I helped Amber plan her wedding, and I think it went very well."

"It was very nice," Kate said. "I'd love for you to help."

Susan turned to Ian. "You're awfully quiet."

Ian sipped his bottled water. "Just taking it all in."

Susan studied Ian for a moment. "Well, I guess there's a lot to take in for such a momentous occasion, isn't there?"

"I fwying!" Violet hollered before standing up on the swing of her swing set.

"Sit down!" Susan barked and rushed over to prevent the birthday girl from taking a trip to the emergency room.

Kate caught the slow, deliberate stride of her parents out of the corner of her eye. They walked side by side, their strides nearly identical, a strange phenomenon given her dad's legs were much longer. "My parents are coming over," she said to Ian under her breath.

Ian straightened and turned to greet them. "Hello, Drs. Lewis."

Her mom flashed a rare smile, seeming pleased that Ian addressed them so formally. "Congratulations, Ian and Kate."

Her dad shook Ian's hand. "Congratulations. Please let us know when the wedding is so we can put it on our calendar."

Which was the happiest they would get.

"Of course we'll let you know," Kate said. "As soon as we know."

"There's too many children here," her mom said, wincing over the noise level. "We only allowed Kate to have one friend over at a time."

Ian pulled Kate close and kissed the top of her head. He knew she'd been lonely as a kid. Her parents were serious academics and pushed her to excel. She'd graduated both high school and college a year ahead of schedule. Most of her childhood had been spent studying.

The children started leaving with their parents, blowing slide whistles from their favor bags in exuberant off-key chaos.

"Oh, thank goodness," her mom said. "Now I can hear myself think."

Kate felt the same way, but it irked her to hear her mom say it. Like she was talking about Kate as a kid. She'd always felt outside of her parents' universe. She wasn't coddled, that was for sure.

"I guess that's our cue," her dad said. "We'd better get on the road."

They turned and left. No hugs. No goodbye.

Ian hugged her as if he knew the lack of affection bothered her. It never had before, but now she'd gotten used to Ian's hugs and *I love you*s and realized her childhood wasn't as normal as she'd once thought. She squeezed him tight.

After all the guests left, she and Ian helped Barry and Amber clean up their house, which was totally trashed—wrapping paper shreds everywhere, chocolate stained the walls (at least she hoped it was chocolate), there was a wet spot on the sofa that she told herself was juice, and someone had emptied both the tissue box and the paper towel roll.

Violet conked out on the sofa, slide whistle clutched in her little hand.

"It'll just be the four of us tonight for your celebration dinner," Amber told them. "Violet's going to have dinner at my friend Steph's house. Her son is three and Violet adores him."

"I hear wedding bells!" Barry said with a laugh.

Ian stiffened.

"Oh, Bare!" Amber exclaimed, tossing an empty paper cup at him. "You're ridiculous. They're preschoolers!"

"Never know," Barry said.

Amber looked to Ian and then to Kate. "You never know. That's the truth."

After they finished cleaning, Kate and Ian went up to the guest room to freshen up before their dinner out. Once she got in the room, she flopped down on the bed, exhausted.

Ian nudged her leg. "When were you going to tell me about Geneva?"

She propped up on her elbows. "When it was definite. It's highly competitive to get time over there."

He sat next to her on the bed. "When will you know?"

"End of May."

"And when do you leave?"

She sat up, crisscrossing her legs. "We could leave together in September. It's for the school year until the following May."

He propped up the pillows and sat, leaning against the headboard. "So another year long distance."

She stared at him, confused. "No, I said together. If we get married this summer, you can live in married housing with me and get health insurance."

"I have health insurance."

"It'll be nice. We won't have to be long distance."

"And what about my job?"

"Could you commute or take a year off?"

"No," he said with an edge to his voice. "I can't commute from Europe, and I can't take a year off."

"But this is a big opportunity for me. I'm close to a breakthrough. This experience could write my ticket to a tenure-level research position anywhere in the world."

"And I'm just supposed to move with you anywhere in the world?"

"Yes!"

"No."

She swallowed over the lump in her throat. "Do you not want to be with me?"

He let out a long breath like he was annoyed or exasperated. She wasn't sure which, but he definitely wasn't happy with her. "I just had a great opportunity come up too as assistant director at the MIT Artificial Intelligence lab."

"Working on robots?"

"Yes. It's a really cool lab with great projects working cross-discipline with designers, engineers, and computer scientists on the cutting edge of AI. And no travel. I can put down roots in Boston."

"Wow! That's great."

He took her hand. "Yes, it is great. It's especially great if you're with me in Boston."

"Well, I don't know. There's fabulous research facilities in California and Chicago too. Not to mention—"

"There's research opportunities in Boston."

She pulled her hand out of his grasp, not liking the sound of this. "So your career takes priority over mine?"

"I didn't say that."

"Then why do I have to choose a job based on where you're at? Why don't you choose a job based on where I'm at?"

"Because we can have both where I'm at."

"So this is the kind of marriage you want?" she asked, her voice rising. "One where I just follow along with whatever you want?"

He jammed a hand through his hair. "Do you have to go to Geneva?"

"No, but I want to." She stood abruptly, her brain whirling through potential futures with Ian. "How exactly do you see our future? Where will we live? Whose career will take precedence? Will we have children? Who will be the caretaker? How will we handle money decisions?"

Ian flopped flat on his back on the bed like she'd knocked him out. "Whoa."

She stood next to the bed and stared down at him. "I want a tenured position at a university. Would you move to where that is?"

He moved to sit on the edge of the bed and patted the spot next to him. "Time for the serious talk."

She sat where he indicated. "Yes."

"There are a lot of universities in Boston," he said.

She tensed, annoyed he kept harping on the same point. She countered with her own repeated point. "There are also wonderful opportunities elsewhere here and abroad."

"And what would I do?"

"Find a job where I am."

"Or…"

She thought about that. "We have a long-distance marriage."

He winced. "That sounds bad."

"Agreed. Your job is more flexible than mine. You can work from home."

"Not with this new job. They need me there. I hoped we'd put down roots in Boston together."

She ground her teeth. She didn't want to fight about this. She wanted Ian on board with her future career. Her mom always said to find a work partner first, life partner second. This was exactly why. She'd worked too hard to just say *whatever you want, honey.*

Maybe she was ill-suited to marriage. Tears unexpectedly stung her eyes. Dammit. She hardly ever cried.

"Kate," Ian said gently. A tear escaped at his caring voice. He wiped her tear with the pad of his thumb. "We'll figure something out. Okay? Don't cry."

"They're happy tears. I'm newly engaged." She sniffled. "Of course I'm very happy."

Ian's lips formed a flat line. He didn't look very happy either.

Barry peeked his head in. "Ready for dinner?"

"Sure," Kate said, leaping to her feet. "Nothing better than a celebratory engagement dinner for two people who are happy to be engaged. Right, Ian?"

He took her hand and squeezed. "Right, Kate."

Barry shot Ian a hard look and then smiled at Kate. "Sure thing. Let's go!"

*So this is awkward.* Ian took a pull on his beer, sitting in a back booth at Garner's Sports Bar & Grill with Kate, Barry, and Amber in an almost solemn occasion for their congratulatory engagement dinner. Kate sat at his side, drinking iced tea, which meant she was pissed and Ian wasn't getting lucky tonight. Not that he really wanted to do anything at his brother's house. When Kate drank beer, it made her extra lusty, so avoiding alcohol at a bar was like holding up a big sign that said *hands off*. Yup, she was pissed he wasn't falling in line with her plan to have a fabulous career with or without him.

Amber broke the awkward silence for the third time. "When we have your engagement party, we'll get it catered by Shane O'Hare. Really gourmet stuff. We figured tonight we'd keep it low key since we have to get Violet soon."

"This is fine," Ian said. He preferred the steak sandwich and fries he'd ordered to fancier stuff. Their food hadn't arrived yet. They'd just been sitting, sorta staring at each other. The dark cherrywood bar to their left was crowded on a Saturday night, and the dining room with a dozen tables and a row of booths was nearly full. The noise level from the bar and the locals' cheerful conversation at nearby tables was a sharp contrast to their quiet group.

Kate nearly vibrated with tension next to him, her back ramrod straight.

Barry's kind brown eyes landed on Kate. "Tell us the latest with your research, Kate."

Kate obligingly launched into a long monologue on her research into the top quark as well as some new discovery in dark matter that delved into some physics Ian was sure no one was following, him included. It didn't help that Kate delivered the information in a tone that lacked all enthusiasm. Amber hid a yawn behind her hand.

Barry nodded and smiled frequently, probably as lost as the rest of them, until Kate finally wound down. Barry turned to Ian. "And how's things in the consulting world?"

"Actually, I might take a job in the AI lab at MIT. One of my old professors wants me to join them as assistant director, working my own research and running the lab. It's really cutting-edge stuff over there."

"That sounds fun," Barry said.

"Yeah." Ian pulled up the lab website on his cell phone and showed everyone the pictures of the AI units for a variety of uses.

"Some of these robots are adorable!" Amber exclaimed. "Like stuffed animals almost."

Ian grinned. "Yeah, filled with machinery. They even have one that helps teach preschoolers foreign languages."

"Wow!" Amber said.

"Very cool," Barry said.

Kate was quiet, staring at the table. He put his cell away.

Another awkward silence fell.

"Is everything okay?" Amber asked, looking from Kate to Ian. "I thought you two would be crazy excited tonight."

Kate spoke in a formal tone. "Barry and Amber, you consider yourself a happily married couple, correct?"

Ian shifted uneasily. The formal tone was a very bad sign. She always got more formal when she was nervous or upset, a callback to her formal upbringing. He hoped she wasn't nervous about them as a couple. He didn't want to break up at their engagement dinner. Or at all.

Barry smiled and put an arm around Amber. "Absolutely."

Amber gazed at Barry adoringly. "Yes. I can't even believe we've already been married four years."

"Feels like four minutes," Barry said, giving her a quick kiss. "Every day is a gift with you, love."

"Oh, Bare," Amber cooed.

Kate cleared her throat loudly. "So my question is, how did you decide whose career comes first?"

Barry and Amber exchanged a look. Amber spoke up. "We both do what we like to do. I paint; Bare does his apps—"

"Don't forget my fro-yo!" Barry said.

"Everyone knows The Dancing Cow," Amber said. "It's your signature."

"And a lot more fun than the software engineering job I used to have," Barry said.

"So everything between your disparate needs and wants worked out on its own?" Kate asked.

"Yeah," Barry and Amber chorused.

"That's no help at all," Kate muttered. "Be specific. How did you decide where to live? Whether or not to have children? Who would care for those children? How do you handle money decisions?"

"Kate," Ian said through his teeth.

Kate glanced at him and turned back to Barry and Amber. "I value your opinion and look to you as a model for a successful relationship. I would really like to hear more about your experience as a happily married couple."

"It was easy," Barry said. "We wanted the same things."

"Oh," Kate said. She turned to Ian. "That's disappointing."

Amber bit back a smile. "You don't need to know how other married couples navigate their relationship, you just need to worry about your own."

"I'm extremely worried," Kate replied. "Ian is acting weird."

Ian glared at her.

"You are," Kate said. "And I don't know what it means, but I don't like it."

Another awkward silence.

Ian took a long drink of beer, avoiding the censure in his brother's eyes. Barry wanted him to step up and fix things, but damn if he knew how. Kate seemed to expect him to go along with whatever she planned for her future. Ian wanted to plan that future in a way that made them both come out a winner. Thankfully their food arrived just then, and they all dug in.

"Oh, hey, there's Daisy!" Amber exclaimed, waving excitedly.

Daisy O'Hare smiled and waved, heading over to their table. Ian had met her a few times. She was one of Amber's close friends, beautiful, blond, and bubbly.

"Hi, guys!" Daisy said, beaming her sunny smile. "Date night?"

"We're celebrating Ian and Kate's engagement!" Amber said brightly. "You remember Bare's brother and my sister?"

"Of course I do!" Daisy exclaimed, taking them in. "Wow. How long's it been? You two haven't changed much."

"Probably four years," Amber said. "They were at our wedding."

"And now you're having your own wedding," Daisy said. "Congratulations! If you want to get married at Ludbury House, you'd better book soon. Shane swore me to secrecy, but—" she lowered her voice and looked around "—Hailey booked a June wedding and a major movie star will be in attendance. They're already talking about security. I'm sure the popularity of Ludbury House will explode after that."

"Oh, wow," Amber said. "I'll call Hailey first thing tomorrow." She turned to Ian and Kate. "That's the wedding planner I told you about."

Kate nodded enthusiastically. Ian kept his mouth shut. He thought it was way too soon to book a venue, not knowing where they'd be a year from now, but this wasn't the time for them to discuss it.

Daisy smiled. "It's so nice you two are getting married. My sister and I married brothers too."

"Keeping it all in the family," Barry said.

"And the kids are close as siblings," Daisy said. "They fight like siblings too."

"Well, they do share a lot of DNA," Barry said.

"True," Daisy replied. "How's Violet?"

"She's great," Amber said. "How's Bryce and Cole?"

"Oh, those two!" Daisy said affectionately. "Rough and

tumble as ever. Now that Bryce is six, he wants to be more like Daddy. He even drove Trav's riding mower, on his own, trying to be a landscaper."

"Ooh, boy!" Barry exclaimed. "Better lock up the machinery."

"We do, but he stole the key," Daisy said. "We've got to be one step ahead of that one. Unfortunately, Cole worships big brother, so that means we have to be twice as vigilant in case of a copycat move."

"Daisy, would you and your husband consider yourself a happily married couple?" Kate asked abruptly.

Ian stifled a groan.

Daisy cocked her head. "Yeah, I would."

"And how long have you been a happily married couple?" Kate asked.

Daisy looked to the ceiling. "I want to say six years." She looked at Kate. "No, Bryce is six, so it must be five years."

"You mean the reverse," Kate said. Ian elbowed her. Kate scooted over like he needed more room. He had to remember she didn't do subtle.

"No, Bryce came first," Daisy said with a laugh. "We did everything backwards, but it all worked out."

Kate pressed on. "May I ask how you decided on careers, child care, and financial decisions?"

Ian dropped his head in his hands.

Daisy laughed. "Trav just wants me to be happy. He's on board for whatever. He's so easygoing. Except when it comes to dinner. I'd better get going. I've got his favorite meatloaf to go."

Ian raised his head. "Bye. Nice to see you."

"Thank you for sharing your marital wisdom," Kate said solemnly.

Daisy exchanged an amused look with Amber. "Sure thing. Good luck!"

Ian turned to Kate once Daisy was out of earshot. "You *have* to stop asking people about their marriage."

Kate huffed. "I'm merely making a scientific inquiry. How else am I supposed to navigate these strange waters?"

"We'll make our own scientific inquiry," he said just to shut the whole embarrassing thing down. "Okay? Just the two of us."

"That would be most satisfactory," Kate replied. She smoothed her hair. "Please excuse my formal tone. This has been a very emotional couple of days." And then she took a sip of his beer, which was a very good sign. Maybe he'd get lucky tonight after all.

Or not.

As soon as he and Kate settled in the guest room that night, she shut the door and locked it. That seemed promising. Since he was already in bed under the covers, he went to strip off his boxer briefs, but she caught the movement and stopped him.

"No. We'll remain dressed for this conversation on our scientific experiment, and I'll remain by the door."

"And then will you join me?" She wore an oversized white T-shirt that was practically see-through and barely covered her ass. He couldn't wait to rip it off her.

"Of course. I need to sleep too." She paced the room, giving him tantalizing glimpses of pink panties, and finally stopped at the foot of the bed. "So we'll be running our own scientific inquiry into marriage. This is very important business. I fear everyone knows the secret but us. How do you suggest we proceed?"

He had no idea.

She scowled. "You just said we'd make a scientific inquiry to shut me up, didn't you?"

"No, no. I really meant it." He thought fast. What would be a reasonable experiment that wouldn't be too difficult? "I was thinking…"

She pushed her glasses in place. "Yes?"

He stacked some pillows behind him and maneuvered to a sitting position, needing the extra time to think. "We need a hypothesis."

"Of course."

He couldn't be too elaborate with the hypothesis since they were mostly long distance. Hmm…

She put her hands on her hips. "I'm getting the feeling you have no more clue than I do, which means we...are... doomed!" That doomed part came out awfully loud.

"Shh, we're not doomed! C'mere, I need a kiss for inspiration."

"You do not! You're trying to short-circuit our conversation." Damn, she was onto him. She started pacing again, muttering to herself. She stopped abruptly, turned to him, and said in a grave voice, "Perhaps I should cancel our experiment."

His stomach dropped. Fuck. He didn't want to hurt her, but he had to be honest. "I'm, uh, not sure I'm ready for marriage. I mean, I hoped we'd get married one day, down the road—"

"So you're calling off the engagement?" she asked in a small voice that made his heart squeeze.

"No," he said quickly. "I just..." Inspiration struck. "Maybe we could do this experiment, and if it goes well, we —" he cleared his throat "—get married sooner, and if it doesn't go the way we hoped, we go back to the long-distance thing." He relaxed a bit. An out clause definitely eased that trapped feeling.

She frowned and sat on the edge of the bed, her hands clasped tightly in her lap.

He joined her, sitting on the edge of the bed, and put his hand on top of hers. "Long distance with the ultimate goal of marriage...down the road."

She turned to him. "I'm confused."

He framed it scientifically to make it clearer for her. "Our hypothesis is that small-scale marriage will be an indicator of large-scale success."

"O-kay," she said slowly, "tell me the rest of the experiment parameters."

"Uh..." *Think!* The pressure of outthinking a brilliant physicist was staggering sometimes. "That means we should do a trial run."

She tilted her head. "I'm intrigued. A trial run to eliminate any doubts of our future together in a permanent commitment."

He focused on the first part because "permanent commitment" was still making him jumpy. "It's a good idea to eliminate any doubts."

"You have doubts."

"Not because of you."

Her blue eyes were direct, pinning him in place. "Then it must be because of you."

"I guess." He swallowed, hating to admit anything that might hurt her, like the fact she'd pulled the lever on the trapdoor the moment she proposed and he'd been in a terrifying free fall ever since. "I love you," he added for good measure.

She sighed. "I love you too. Back to the experiment. When shall we begin?"

"When do you have time off?"

"I can move in with you for the entire month of May. Two weeks of vacation, two weeks of working off-site. I've been wanting to focus more on data analysis."

Whoa. A whole month. They'd only ever been together two weeks max. He pushed the panicky trapped feeling down. It was only two weeks more than their longest visit. Surely he could manage that. And he had an out clause. They could always go back to their long-distance relationship. This was really a win-win.

"Great!" he exclaimed, putting as much enthusiasm into it as a fiancé should. Technically they were still engaged, and he couldn't bear to tell her differently so soon after her heartfelt proposal. "We'll try living together then. See how it goes." He relaxed. Yes, this was a good idea. A trial run.

"Ian," she said softly.

He pushed a lock of soft blond hair back from her face. "What?"

She stared straight ahead. "At the conclusion of this experiment, will you be breaking up with me?"

"Kate! Of course not."

She turned to him, a puzzled look on her face. "Then

what's the point if you've already concluded we'll be together?"

"It's just a question of when. Right? Should we let the relationship go on longer before tying the knot?"

She nodded once. "Perhaps some compatibility testing is in order."

"Already compatible."

She huffed. "If we're not going to do this scientifically, then I don't see the point."

"Okay, okay."

She stood and paced by the foot of the bed before finally saying in a grave tone, "I'll research major issues in marriage, and then I'll construct an experiment, which we'll do during our trial run of living together."

Well, that was a helluva lot easier than *him* coming up with something. He was sure she'd find a flaw in any scientific experiment he devised. Give him coding any day.

"That works," he said, earning one of her rare beaming smiles. "Let's keep it just between us, okay?"

"Of course," she replied. "We don't want outside influences to hinder the results."

"I'm sure we'll pass with flying colors."

"Please try to be objective."

"I'll be completely objective," he said solemnly.

She held up a finger. "Like an experiment on two chimps in love that you've never met. No preconceived judgments on either chimp."

"Sure."

Two chimps doing the chimp love thing? Primal animal heat. Yup. Buckle up for a fun ride!

**5**

———————

*Let me off this thing!*

Kate was scaring the bejeezus out of him and it wasn't even nine a.m. They were driving over to Ludbury House with Amber to meet with the wedding planner, which would've been terrifying all on its own, but then Kate was telling him and Amber all about the twenty journal articles on positive marriage outcomes in America she'd already book-marked for the experiment. She was tossing out scary words like "transactional analysis" and "differentiation," and he was desperately trying to steer the conversation to absolutely anything else. The weather, the Sox, Violet, even physics fell flat.

Kate didn't steer easily.

Or at all.

Amber had announced the wedding planner appointment at breakfast, and then Kate had informed everyone that it was a practical thing to do regardless of their experimental outcome since they were only in town for the weekend.

Amber had laughed. Barry shot Ian a questioning look.

"Don't ask," Ian said. The rest had been a blur of excited sister talk that he hadn't had the heart to stomp on with a reminder of his and Kate's agreement from last night. He told himself this would just be an exploratory outing. Kate was a practical woman. She understood they would still have a trial run before anything definite was planned.

Now Amber parked, and they all got out of the car at Ludbury House. Kate lagged behind, reading on her cell phone, muttering about a newly discovered mathematical equation of love.

"This is her version of wedding planning," Amber told him with a smile. "She brings a scientific point of view to everything."

"I don't think love is scientific," he confided.

"Untrue," Kate said, surprising him. He thought she was thoroughly immersed in her love equation. "There have been numerous scientific studies on chemistry, relationships, and marital outcomes."

He crossed back to Kate, took her hand, and brushed his lips across her knuckles. Her eyes snapped to his, her jaw dropping.

He smiled and pressed under her chin, closing her mouth. "At least you know we have chemistry."

"That's one of the key indicators of long-term relationship success," she said in a breathy voice.

He cupped her jaw, tilted her head up, and watched her eyes flutter closed. He pressed his lips to hers gently. "It's fun too."

"Come on, you two," Amber called over her shoulder. "We don't want to be late."

They caught up with Amber and crossed from the back parking lot around to the front door of what locals called "the mansion." It was an impressive building, a sprawling two-and-a-half-story white clapboard house with white columns and a wraparound porch. It was a former estate, owned by the town of Clover Park, and used for community events and weddings.

Ian stepped ahead of the women and opened the heavy wooden door for them. He joined them in a large two-story foyer with a crystal chandelier and, beyond that, a huge staircase.

"Welcome to Ludbury House!" a woman exclaimed,

rushing to greet them from where she must've been waiting in a room next to the foyer. She had long, wavy light red hair, pale blue eyes, and a form-fitting green dress showing off a killer body. Not that he noticed stuff like that anymore. "I'm Hailey Adams, your wedding planner! You must be Ian, Kate, and Amber!"

"That's right," Amber said.

Hailey beamed. "Right this way!" She gestured with an enthusiastic wave of her hand and turned on her high heels toward the back of the house. They followed her to a large empty ballroom with a table and chairs set directly in the center under an elaborate gold and crystal chandelier.

"Have a seat," Hailey said, gesturing to the red velvet cushioned chairs at the table. "I'll be right back."

They settled at the table to wait. Amber and Kate admired a vase full of red and pink flowers on the table. Ian stared at three white binders that gave him hives. That looked like a lot of planning, a lot of decisions, and a definite outlay of money that made the trapped feeling worse. This appointment had probably been a mistake.

Hailey returned, holding a small rose corsage in a plastic container. "So which one is the bride?"

Kate raised her hand, her expression serious like they were in school.

"Then this is for you!" Hailey exclaimed. She pulled the red rose with baby's breath out of the container and pinned it to Kate's blue sweater.

"Congratulations, Kate!" Hailey exclaimed.

Kate stared at the corsage.

Hailey took her seat across from them and set a few business cards on the table. "We're meeting in the center of the ballroom because I want you to feel what it'll be like when you're the center of attention at the reception." She smiled at Kate. "Every bride is special at Ludbury House." At Kate's continued silent staring at her corsage, Hailey gave her a look of concern. "Are you okay?"

Kate met Hailey's eyes with an expression of wonder. "I've never had a corsage before."

Ian's chest clutched. Kate had missed out on so much with her strict formal upbringing. She hadn't gone to prom or any other dance for that matter. Never even dated before he hooked up with her that first time. He took her hand and squeezed. This appointment hadn't been a mistake. Kate deserved to feel special, whether or not they waited to get married a comfortable distance down the road.

Kate gazed at him, her eyes a little glassy. "It's starting to feel real now," she said hoarsely.

Ian turned to Hailey. "Give the bride whatever she wants."

Amber sucked in an audible breath.

He'd eat ramen noodles for a year if that was what it took to come up with the money. Nothing mattered except Kate having her moment.

"Ian," Kate whispered, "we haven't even completed our experiment yet."

"I'm postulating the results will be positive," he returned, trying to sound as scientific as possible.

"Well, I don't know," Kate said. "I still think an experiment will be worthwhile."

"You can do your experiment and plan your wedding at the same time," Amber put in.

Kate studied her sister and slowly smiled. "Okay."

"Wonderful!" Hailey exclaimed. "This will be so fun. Kate, tell me how you imagined your big day."

Kate got a dreamy, faraway look, a wistful smile playing over her lips. "It's a little out there," she whispered.

"We want this to be your dream wedding," Hailey said, leaning across the table eagerly. "Tell me absolutely everything."

Pink tinged Kate's cheeks, and she looked over at Amber. "It's kinda over the top."

"Now you have to say it," Amber said with a grin. "You can't tease us and not spill."

Hailey nodded and smiled encouragingly at Kate.

"Whatever you want," Ian said, though he really hoped it

wasn't physics related. Or some kind of sci-fi theme. He wasn't so into a *Star Trek* wedding.

Kate wound a lock of hair around her finger, took a deep breath, and then confessed her dream wedding, shocking him. It sounded like a fairy tale. Kate described herself wearing a puffy white gown, gloves up to her elbows, tiara, and silver shoes with crystals. Him in a tux with top hat and tails. Ballroom dancing by candlelight. The two of them leaving in a horse-drawn carriage. It occurred to him that he'd merely scratched the surface with getting to know his fascinating girlfriend. A serious physicist with secret romantic longings. The cool thing was the more he got to know her, the deeper he fell in love.

He tuned out when Hailey cracked open the first binder full of pictures and described all the possibilities for the ceremony, catering, flowers, cake, music, and transportation. He kept his gaze fixed on Kate, glowing and happy, as she pointed to pictures of things she liked. This was all that mattered. A happy Kate.

An hour later, the binders closed, and he realized all eyes were on him. "What?"

"She wants us to set a date," Kate said.

"Oh. But we haven't…" He pulled at the collar of his shirt, suddenly choking him. "We, uh, don't know about your fellowship yet." *Or whether we'll be long distance for another year.*

"Can we get back to you in May?" Kate asked. "That's when I hear if I'll be in Geneva next fall."

Hailey shook her head. "I have to warn you, I have a huge wedding planned this June. Major, major press will be in attendance. I fully expect Ludbury House to become a wedding destination. If you don't book today, I can't promise I'll have the date you want in the future."

Ian broke out in a sweat. He didn't want to tell Kate no after all this planning stuff, but this felt so sudden. So locked in.

Kate and Amber exchanged a concerned look.

"August?" Kate asked him.

He opened his mouth and closed it again. That was only five months away. The walls were closing in on him. He went hot and then cold.

"Ian?" Kate prompted.

"I have cold feet," he blurted. "Nothing personal, Kate."

"Of course not," Kate said. "I'm the bride. Why would I take it personally that the groom has cold feet?"

Amber laughed and then slapped a hand over her mouth.

Hailey bared her teeth at him. "Cold feet are my specialty," she said in a near growl.

Kate stood. "Ian, let's go. We will proceed with our experiment as planned." Uh-oh, the formal tone was back. His cold feet had triggered her cold feet. Now she had doubts about them.

He stood and reached for Kate's hand, but she moved out of his reach and snagged a business card from the table. Ian knew he was in trouble now. He had to prove himself with whatever scientific torture Kate devised, get over his own damn cold feet, and make her dreams come true.

Kate scanned the business card and turned to Hailey. "Thank you, Hailey Adams, Love Junkie, we'll be in touch."

He glanced at the card. It actually said that, silver bells embossed on a card with Hailey Adams, Love Junkie.

As soon as they were outside, he tried to reassure Kate. "I'll get there. I just need a little time."

"We shall see," she replied ominously.

Kate reported on the decline of marriage in America on the drive home, Amber kept giggling, and Ian sank deeper into his seat.

~

"How'd it go?" Barry asked the moment Kate, Amber, and Mr. Cold Feet stepped in the door.

"Ian has cold feet," Kate informed him. She was pissed at Ian for revealing this sad state of affairs in front of the wedding planner after more than an hour of planning for a wedding that might never happen. This was so embarrassing.

Why didn't he just say he didn't want to go to the wedding planning appointment? Communication was vitally important in a marriage. Theirs sucked.

"Kate has a Cinderella fantasy," Ian returned.

Grrr...Kate wanted to kick him in the shin, but she was too mature for such childish behavior.

Amber threw her arms over both of their shoulders. "Play nice, children."

Barry shook his head. "Sorry I missed it. Sounds like it must've been a hoot."

"Oh, we hooted, all right," Amber said. "Where's Vi?"

"She's watching TV in our room," Barry said. "She's running a low-grade fever. I'm not sure if she's sick or just teething. Could be her two-year molars are coming in."

Amber raced upstairs.

Barry gave Kate a sympathetic look. "Anything I can do?"

"Any advice?" Kate asked.

He glanced at his brother. "For getting over cold feet? Time."

"I told you I just needed some time," Ian muttered.

"For marriage," Kate said. "Any advice for a successful marriage?"

Barry rubbed his chin thoughtfully. Kate held her breath. Communication? Differentiation combined with involvement? Positive feedback loops? Mutually enjoyable activities? She just needed a direction. They could work on it if they knew what "it" was. Even Ian seemed riveted with anticipation.

"Sex," Barry pronounced. "Lots and lots of sex."

"We're golden," Ian said with a big smile.

The brothers exchanged an enthusiastic high five.

"Men!" Kate threw up her hands and stomped upstairs.

**6**

---

"I'm taking the job in the AI lab," Ian announced, startling Kate.

It was Thursday, their last day in Boston, and they were having a lunch of grilled cheese sandwiches in his apartment. Somehow during this busy week with Ian showing her the sights, Kate had managed to push his job offer and their diverging future career paths from her mind. Now it was like a Boston cream pie in the face. Unavoidably needing to be dealt with and very messy.

Kate peeled the crust off her sandwich, waffling between irritated that he hadn't asked her opinion on his job decision and pleased that he was communicating with her as was recommended in the successful relationship literature.

Ian went on. "I'm signing the employee agreement and emailing Dr. Wilson after lunch."

Again, no question. More of an announcement. Kate set her sandwich down. "So you're just telling me this, not asking me."

"I'm keeping you in the loop."

"So now we know you'll be rooted in Boston and I have no choice but to follow along with your decision."

Ian's kind brown eyes studied her for a moment. "The AI lab gave me a week to think it over, and I think it's a good fit.

I have to give them an answer today. Tomorrow we're flying to Chicago."

"Yes, of course." Kate reached for composure. Everything Ian said was true and logical, so there was really no reason to be irritated. She should possibly be thanking him for keeping her in the loop and praising his open communication. She opened her mouth to do exactly that, but what came out was, "Excuse me. I need to do some research."

She stood with her plate and glass.

"You didn't finish your sandwich," Ian said.

"I'm not hungry."

"Kate."

She looked at a point over his shoulder. "What?"

"Are you upset?"

She checked in with herself. Upset? Irritated? Angry? None of these emotions swirling through her made any sense. The facts were simple—Ian must give an answer to the job offer. And he must always choose what was right for his career just as she must always choose what was right for her career, even if those decisions put them on opposite sides of the Atlantic Ocean.

Of course, she hadn't landed the fellowship in Geneva yet. Maybe they'd just be thousands of miles of land apart. Or maybe they wouldn't be apart at all. But would that be caving in to what he wanted? Did she have a clear enough head to make her own career decisions for what was best for her as he did so easily just now?

"Kate?" Ian prompted.

"I'm not sure," she replied. She wrapped her sandwich and stuck it in the refrigerator. Then she set the dishes in the sink.

Ian's arms slid around her waist from behind.

"When do you start?" she asked.

He kissed her temple. "Probably three weeks. I've got this next week off to spend with you, and then I'll give two weeks' notice at my old job."

She pulled away. "I really need to do some research." The urgent need to scour the marriage literature on two-career families made her rush to the living room and grab her laptop.

"Okay," Ian said easily. Thankfully, he was completely oblivious to her distress. She didn't want to be that awful girlfriend who tried to hold their boyfriend back from great things. She wanted to treat Ian the way she wanted to be treated—with complete respect for the wisdom of her decisions.

Yet when she pulled open her laptop, the journal articles she bookmarked swam before her eyes because in making his career decision, he'd just put limits on hers.

She took off her glasses and quickly wiped her eyes. She shoved the glasses back in place and took a deep breath, forcing herself to focus on marriage research. Her experiment was more critical than ever. Their future depended on it.

Kate dove in and didn't come up for air until Ian waved a hand in front of her face. "Hey," he said, "let's go grab a bite for dinner."

She started and checked the time on her laptop. It was after six. She hadn't realized she'd been immersed in the marriage literature for so long. She'd also constructed a useful compatibility quiz drawn from several relationship-savvy websites such as *Cosmo* and *Glamour*. She'd found *Cosmo* to be most informative on several levels of pleasing your man in areas she'd thought about—sex—and areas she hadn't even considered such as skincare, an inviting living space, and gestures of love. She hoped there was an equivalent magazine geared toward pleasing your woman. She'd research that at the very next opportunity.

Ian took her hand and pulled her up from the sofa. "You get a lot of work done?"

"Yes. It was a most productive session."

"Great." He framed her face with both hands and kissed her tenderly. Her throat got tight as all the emotions she'd pushed down returned at the warm look in his eyes. "So we good?"

She couldn't speak, so she tried to nod, but even that was impossible with the way he held her head. His hands slid into her hair and she felt her hair loosen and then fall from its messy half ponytail half bun.

Ian dipped his head and nuzzled into her neck, bringing hot shivers of pleasure, before moving up to her ear. "Good enough for a quick trip to the bedroom before dinner?" he asked in a husky coaxing voice.

Her stomach growled, speaking for her. She'd never finished her lunch.

Ian laughed and met her eyes. "Your stomach has spoken. Let's go."

They had a hearty dinner at her favorite Boston restaurant, Sweet Cheeks, where she indulged in fried buttermilk chicken with mac n' cheese. The cheerful busy place made it easy to forget her worries over their future. Ian was in good spirits over his new job and how enthusiastic his new boss was to have him join the group. She told herself everything would work out as it should.

That little mantra worked all the way until four a.m. when she woke from a vivid dream where Ian was pulling her arm in one direction and her research director, Dr. Weintraub, dressed improbably in her hydrogen costume, pulled her other arm in the opposite direction. She jackknifed up in bed with a harsh gasp just as she was about to be torn in two.

Ian slept soundly at her side, naked from their earlier activities and lying on his back in his open trusting way. She'd read just this afternoon that sleeping on your back was a trusting position and sleeping on your stomach was a defensive position. Kate had purposely tried to switch from stomach sleeping to back sleeping and look what it got her—a nightmare.

"Ian," she whispered, curling up against his side. No response. She rested her head on his chest and listened to the reassuring thud of his heartbeat. Her own rapid heartbeat slowed, and her mind cleared. She lifted her head. "Are you awake?"

Silence. She kissed him, hoping to stir him, but he kept right on sleeping. She pulled the blanket off him and settled herself on top of him. His body heat would be more than enough to keep them both warm. She wiggled a little, fitting herself better against him. This was nice. He was so warm, and skin on skin always made her feel so alive. The nightmare slipped fully from her mind, and she relaxed, resting her cheek against his chest.

A few moments later, he said, "Mmm…" the sound reverberating through his chest, and he wrapped his arm around her waist. Oh, good, he was waking up.

She lifted her head. "I've constructed a ten-part compatibility quiz."

"Morning," he mumbled.

She brightened. "Morning! Even though I haven't finished designing the scientific experiment for our trial run, I thought maybe we could do the quiz as a precursor. The initial results could prove useful in experiment design."

One of his eyes opened. "Dark," he muttered, closing his eye. "Time is it?"

She glanced at the clock that read 4:05 and quickly decided not to answer the question directly. She really wanted to get started on finding the answers she needed to their future sooner rather than later. "It's morning," she assured him. "Would you prefer to spend a Saturday relaxing at home, hiking in the wilderness, or at a blow-out bash on your friend's killer yacht?"

He groaned.

Undeterred, she broke it down for him to make answering as easy as possible. "Would you prefer to spend a Saturday relaxing at home?"

He let out a small sigh that might've been a snore.

She quickly blurted the rest of the question, "Or would you rather hike or party? Personally I'd choose…oh, wait. I'm not supposed to share until I hear your answer so you won't be biased. Couples tend to want to agree to avoid confrontation, but since we're just beginning what should be a truly objective—"

She squeaked. Ian had unexpectedly flipped her onto her back. Before she could continue their admittedly one-sided conversation, he was on top of her. His fingers speared into her hair, and then his mouth shifted to kiss along her neck. Her lips parted on a sigh as she melted into the mattress. He nipped at her neck, and she jolted at the sharp electric pleasure. His warm lips skimmed along the sensitive skin on the underside of her jaw and then to the soft spot just below her ear.

She wrapped her arms around his neck, sifting her fingers through his soft hair. "Were you using my short circuit to make me be quiet?"

He tugged her earlobe between his teeth, giving her a hot shiver. Her eyes fluttered closed.

"Ian," she whispered.

His mouth grazed her earlobe as he spoke, sending more hot shivers through her. "No, I love when you talk." His voice was silky. "Keep talking."

He kissed his way down her body, his lips like warm velvet across her collarbone, her chest, and then to her breast, where he lingered, kissing and tasting in ever-tightening spirals. All thoughts of compatibility testing fled. His finger flicked across her beaded nipple, making her gasp. He lowered his head, his mouth closing around her nipple and sucking hard. A rush of heat surged between her legs. Her lips parted on a moan, and she moved her hips restlessly against him. He lifted his body and slid his hand between her legs in one long heavy stroke as he shifted his mouth to her other breast, suckling hard.

"Please, please," she chanted.

He lifted his head. "Keep talking, sweetheart." His fingers slid inside her, thrusting in and out, and he resumed suckling her aching, tingling breast, causing a sharp need that could not be denied.

She raised her hips. "Take me. I need you." He made her crazy. Absolutely crazy.

"I want to hear you talk some more." He stroked her lazily between the legs. "I love when you talk. Let's hear you begging."

She smacked his shoulder. "Ian! I'm not begging. Just give it to me."

"Give you what?" he drawled.

She was about to reply when he suddenly levered his body lower, his lips landing on her belly, where he licked her belly button in one long sweep. A full-body shudder ripped through her because she knew where this was going.

"Open your legs nice and wide," he said in a low gravelly voice.

She did, her breath ragged, her body humming with anticipation. His warm lips grazed along her inner thigh, and she bit her lip to stop herself from begging.

"So quiet now," he murmured, moving to kiss along the inside of her other thigh, so damn close to where she wanted him.

"Please!" she begged.

"There she is," he said, pushing her legs over his shoulders, leaving her open and exposed to his wicked tongue. His hands slid under her bottom, lifting her to the angle he wanted.

"Please," she whispered.

He dipped his head, gave her one long stroke and then sucked hard, sending shockwaves of sensation through her. She cried out, and he gentled. "Oh-oh-oh," she said as he lapped at her.

He lifted his head, his voice rough. "Keep talking."

She did. She couldn't help herself. "Don't stop, don't stop, don't stop…" she chanted. And then she was overwhelmed and quieted, so-so close. She trembled as he held her on the sharp edge of release. He knew her well, knew when to push hard and when to pull back. She whimpered incoherently. He pushed her hard suddenly, his mouth firm and hungry on her, and she exploded in a hot rush. He stayed with her, letting her ride out every wave of pleasure until she was spent.

A slow satisfied smile bloomed as she floated in a haze, vaguely aware of Ian shifting away. He cupped her between the legs suddenly in a possessive hold. She jolted and moaned. And then he was on top of her, lifting her legs high around his waist and thrusting deep.

"Yes!" she hissed.

His fingers entwined with hers, pressing her hands to the mattress on either side of her head. He nipped her bottom lip, and his tongue thrust inside her mouth, igniting her. She moaned as he thrust hard and deep, over and over, the sweet pressure building and building and building.

He tore his mouth away and rasped, "I'm hitting a ten tonight."

He was always a ten on her performance-rating scale—thickness, check; dexterity, check; reciprocity, double check; alpha-level dominance, yeah, baby! But she let him make an effort anyway.

She concentrated on sounding casual. "You're nearly there."

"Nearly!" He pulled out, flipped her over, yanked her hips up, and plunged deep. *Yes!* His hand snaked around, stroking her the way that made her eyes roll back in her head. "Now where are we at, Kate?"

She panted and trembled under him, completely beyond speech.

He got rougher, pushing her harder, taking her deep. She shook with need, heart-pounding exhilaration racing through her. "Where we at?" he growled. "Say it."

"Ten!" she shouted before shuddering in a climax so hard she saw the entire galaxy of stars flash before her eyes.

"Damn right," he growled before sinking his teeth into the cord of her neck like an animal as he thrust for his own release. She trembled under him. He sent her over again, tumbling along with him as he exploded inside her.

He held her tightly, buried deep as they both panted in the aftermath. She found herself beaming for no other reason than the universe was a beautiful place, and they were one hundred percent compatible in a very important, thoroughly satisfying area.

"Our compatibility in the bedroom is a key factor in positive marriage outcomes," she informed him once she could speak.

He pulled out and crashed to the bed beside her, rolling to his back. She cuddled up against him.

Her mind reached back to the five main factors she'd discovered and, since she was sure he was now fully awake, she confidently broached the topic that would be the cornerstone of her experiment. "There are other factors, of course, *mrwmph*." Ian's mouth covered hers, and she lost her train of thought.

He broke the kiss, rolling to his side and pulling her leg over his hip, bringing them into full-body contact.

She tried to focus again. "For example—"

He thrust his leg between hers, applying just enough pressure to her still-tingling sex that her thoughts scattered like photons. Distracting sparks of pleasure radiated through her. His large hand cupped the back of her neck as he spoke near her ear in a deep husky voice. "Maybe we could add to the experiment, try some new things."

A full-body shiver ran through her both from the sexy voice and the fact that he was speaking her scientific language. "Yes," she whispered.

"Good," he crooned, his hand sliding down her spine and resting just above her bottom.

She moaned, extremely distracted and entirely too needy for someone that had just been thoroughly satisfied. Before she could find the words to continue their conversation, he went on, his deep rumble in her ear bringing more hot tingles of excitement.

"For future experimentation, how do you feel about being tied up?"

"You know I enjoy alpha-level dominance," she replied immediately. "It's one of the key factors in my rating system."

He groaned against her neck, the vibrations flooding her with pleasure as much as his words. "Wrists and ankles, spread-eagled for as long as I like."

She shivered in his arms. "Definitely add that to the experiment. We simply won't know until we try."

He palmed her ass. "We might have to try several times to be sure."

"It's all in the name of science!" she squeaked. She barely knew what she was saying, she was so turned on.

He chuckled and kissed her. "Anything in the name of science."

Those words rang so true to her scientific mind that a sense of peace washed over her, relaxing her and making her drowsy.

"Sleep now," he murmured. "I'll experiment with you later."

Those sweet words sent her into a deep dreamless sleep.

She woke when Ian shook her by the shoulder. She opened her eyes to find him standing next to the bed, fully dressed. "We overslept," he said. "Hurry and pack or we'll miss our flight."

And just like that, it was back to reality. One that she wasn't so sure she was equipped to deal with. Some part of her wished they could just stay in bed, where everything between them worked perfectly. Besides, he'd revved her up good last night, and she could easily do another round.

She sat up. His back was to her as he yanked clothes out of the dresser and tossed them in a duffle bag. "How about a quickie?"

He slowly turned and gave her a hot look that had her spirits lifting. "Get ready fast, and I'll initiate you into the mile-high club on the plane."

Her eyes narrowed. "Are you already a member?"

He grinned. "Nope. I just like to initiate you."

He was referring to his initiating her into the world of pleasure when he took her virginity. Or maybe when he initiated her into oral sex. Or full-tilt boogie orgasms. He really did like to initiate her. And she really did like to be initiated.

"Okay." She stood, grabbed some clothes, and headed for a quick shower. When she returned to the bedroom, freshly clean and dressed, Ian had already packed her bag for her.

He grabbed her around the waist and pulled her in for a quick kiss. "Mile-high club, here we come!"

**7**

———

The mile-high club was out of reach by a mile.

Unfortunately for Ian, the plane was small, two rows of two-seaters, and completely packed. No fooling around under a blanket would be possible, and the restroom appeared to be permanently *occupado*.

*They'd had a good run,* Ian thought morosely. Without his go-to sexy weapon of distraction, Kate was like a hamster on the talk-about-the-relationship wheel. He fidgeted in his seat and tried unsuccessfully to stretch out his long legs. The trapped feeling was even worse with his long frame squeezed into a coach seat between the window and the inquiring Kate. God forbid he didn't answer her question right. Then it was, *brrapp.* Big old *wrong answer* face.

"If I bought you an engagement ring, would you wear it?" she asked once she secured her lap tray into the upright position. They'd just finished a tiny potato chip snack during which the questions had blessedly stopped. He kinda wanted to ask the flight attendant for seconds on the snack.

"We should probably save our money for a house," he said quite reasonably.

She was quiet. He looked over to find her scowling. *Brrapp.* Wrong answer.

"Yes, I'd wear it," he amended.

Still scowling. He was terrible at these high-stakes question games.

"How about I get you an engagement ring instead?" he asked.

"You should save your money for my Cinderella fantasy." Her tone was flat. He couldn't tell if it was a dig at him teasing her for it or if she really meant it. This sarcasm thing was new on her, and it popped up here and there, but nothing consistent. The female mind had never been so unclear.

"Okay," he said slowly. Then he turned the question thing around. Let her answer high-stakes questions instead. "Are you happy to be engaged?"

She pinned him with a hard look. "Are *you* happy to be engaged?"

"I'm happy when you're happy," he answered honestly.

Kate scowled at him. *Brrapp.* Wrong answer. "Great."

"That was sarcasm, right?"

She huffed and rolled her eyes.

"Hey, now, where did this come from?" he asked. "Why are you suddenly sarcastic?"

She lifted a shoulder up and down. "I don't know. Maybe it's the lunch crew. They're big on that."

"The lunch crew?"

"Yeah, the guys I have lunch with every day."

"You have lunch with a bunch of guys every day?"

"Yeah."

"How long has this been going on? And why didn't you tell me?"

She wrapped a lock of blond hair around her finger and faced front. "Since January."

"It's March now. Why didn't you mention it?"

"I don't know. I guess because you and I were so busy, *you know*, I never thought of it."

He leaned close. "We don't always *you know*. Friday night is for *you know*. Sunday night is for real conversation." They'd made a schedule for their long-distance relationship, at Kate's insistence, and Friday night was for phone sex, Sunday night was for talking.

"I know," she said, "but on Sunday I'm still thinking about Friday. It's fun." She turned to him and grinned.

His heart squeezed. Honestly, Kate was amazing him lately. She never used to talk about having fun. He had to encourage her to have fun.

He tilted her chin up and gave her a quick kiss. "I can't wait to meet your new friends."

"Only if there's no male territorial posturing."

He beat his chest like a gorilla.

She giggled.

He took her hand and entwined his fingers with hers.

"Do you trust me?" she asked.

"Yes."

She beamed. *Right answer.*

"I'm very popular with the guys now that I'm taken," she informed him.

He did a double take. "What?"

She snort-laughed. "It's true. Nate says it's because the pressure's off, and they don't have to impress me. So they're just being themselves. And I told them being themselves is wonderful, and now they all kind of adore me."

He pulled his hand free from hers, rubbed his forehead, and contemplated why Kate had never mentioned this adoring thing before. He didn't want to come off like a jealous boyfriend, but...he was a jealous boyfriend. "So you like having a group of guys adore you?"

"Yeah, it's never happened before." She kept right on smiling. Like it was perfectly fine to tell your fiancé that a group of guys spent every lunch break flirting with you. They were twentysomething physicists too. Just her type.

But wait. A flicker of hope went up. Maybe she'd misread the situation. It wouldn't be the first time. "And how do you know they adore you?" he asked.

"Nate told me."

He plowed a hand through his hair. "What? When did this happen? Tell me exactly what he said."

"I thought you trusted me. Why all the questions?"

"Just answer the last one."

"Five Fridays ago."

"Not that question. Tell me exactly what he said."

"That's not a question. Your last question was when did this happen?"

"Kate," he said through his teeth.

Kate pulled her cell phone from her purse and tapped it. "There, see, exactly what he said."

A text from Nate Patel. She showed him the screen. *The guys adore you. We're so glad you joined us for lunch. Remember us when you get your Nobel Prize.*

Oh fuck. He could read between the lines. This wasn't "the guys" who adored Kate. This was Nate. Nate adored her. Nate was glad she joined him for lunch.

Nate was about to meet his competition.

Ian was in shock. The first time he'd met Kate and her fellow physicists at last year's holiday party, she'd been very much apart from her peers. In fact, most of the physicists had been standing around the party room awkwardly, but now, it was like Kate was the sun and they revolved around her. She sat at a circular table in the cafeteria, and the men, four of them, sat around it, riveted on her every word. It was clear they respected her insights as a physicist as they shared with her their experimental findings, eager to hear her thoughts. But it was more than that. Kate was lit from within as she not only talked about physics, but also made sarcastic remarks that the men found quite amusing.

Well, guess what? Guys didn't laugh that much unless they were into a girl. Sure, Ian had always thought her beautiful, but it wasn't something that hit you all at once. You had to look beyond the big tortoiseshell glasses and messy bun of blond hair, intuit what was hiding under her baggy sweaters. But not anymore. It wasn't that she'd changed her look, not at all, but she'd changed her focus. Instead of being in her head, focused on her work, she'd learned to shut that part down during breaks and focus outward on her male peers.

Who clearly worshiped her.

There was Nate Patel, the adoring physicist. Ian was confident enough in his masculinity to admit that Nate was good-looking with short dark brown hair with some spikes in front, deep brown eyes, smooth light brown skin, and a stunning white-toothed smile. Strike one. He was a snappy dresser in a crisp white button-down shirt, perfectly ironed gray pants and leather shoes, like he'd just stepped out of *GQ* magazine. Strike two. Nate had a slight exotic accent and a melodic charming voice that he used to great effect on Kate. And he wore spicy cologne. Strike one million and—

Kate threw her head back and laughed. "Oh, Nate, you're so funny."

*Huff, huff.* Ian was funny too.

There was also Colt, who had a California surfer vibe with shaggy dirty blond hair, blue eyes, and a head full of dark matter studies. Ty, who seemed to be emulating Nate with similar clothes right down to the leather shoes. They even had the same haircut, though Ty's hair was light brown, and, frankly, he still looked a little gangly and awkward. And, finally, Ian's favorite for being the least threat in the attractiveness realm was Mike, who had greasy hair, a stained T-shirt, and ripped jeans.

When he'd first met everyone where they met up at Kate's office, Kate had introduced him. Right away, he knew Nate would be trouble.

"This is Dr. Ian Furnukle," Kate said, "my boyfriend. He's also a computer scientist with a special interest in artificial intelligence."

He was greeted with an assortment of muttered "nice to meet yous" from the guys, except Nate, who gave him a firm handshake.

"So you're real," Nate said with a big flashy smile. "We were beginning to think you were an imaginary boyfriend."

Kate laughed. "Oh, Nate, you crack me up!"

Nate turned a full-wattage smile on Kate. "Su-u-u-re, your boyfriend from Boston who no one has ever seen and you have no pictures of. S-u-u-re—" he widened his eyes "—he's real."

Kate's sarcasm influence was suddenly clear.

"Ha-ha-ha-ha!" Kate put her hands on her hips, making her breasts thrust forward, and shook her head, loosening her hair. A lock of hair fell out of her bun and curled near her cheek.

Ian didn't miss Nate admiring that tousled sexy look.

"I'm very real," Ian said.

No response from the group. Ian was invisible.

Things went downhill from there. Ian was the unwanted shadow behind Kate's sun.

Now he was finishing up a dry ham and cheese sandwich, trying to figure out how to neutralize the threat to his girlfriend without coming off like a jealous jerk. Very fine line he was walking here.

A middle-aged bald man stopped by their table. "Hi, everyone. Kate, so glad to have you back."

Kate straightened and pushed up her glasses. "Hello, Dr. Weintraub."

"No need to be so formal. You can call me Gary."

"This is Dr. Furnukle, my guest for the week," Kate said, becoming even more formal. She must be nervous. "Dr. Furnukle, this is Dr. Weintraub, the director of our research program."

Ian shook his hand. "Hi, I'm Ian. Nice to meet you."

Dr. Weintraub smiled widely. "Oh, you must be the boyfriend. Kate mentioned you when she returned to work after the New Year, and she's been in a good mood since. It's been a boon to her research, actually, so thank you for making her so happy."

Kate smiled tightly.

"I aim to please," Ian said. "Kate and I go way back."

"Our mutual siblings are married," Kate said.

Dr. Weintraub leaned close to Ian and spoke in a conspiratorial tone. "Whatever you're doing, keep it up. Kate's near a breakthrough. If we can run some tests to prove her theory, she could earn the next Nobel Prize in physics."

Ian's jaw dropped. A Nobel Prize? For real? At twenty-five?

"Hear, hear!" Nate said, clanging his spoon against his glass of peach iced tea.

Kate tittered and smoothed her hair. "Well, we don't know that for sure. There's still much work to be done."

"It's true," Dr. Weintraub said. "I want to look over your fellowship application before you send it out. Can you have it by Wednesday?"

"Yes," Kate replied. "I already know what I want to say, it's just a matter of gathering all my materials."

Dr. Weintraub looked pleased. "Good." He turned to Ian. "We're trying to keep the details of her research on the down low. Sometimes new discoveries happen in two places at the same time, a parallel discovery phenomenon, and we're eager to have Kate's results published first."

"Of course," Ian said. He felt like an idiot. Kate had told him how important her research was, how much the Geneva fellowship meant to her, and he never wanted to hold her back, but he had no idea she was that big of a deal. A Nobel Prize-winning physicist?

Dr. Weintraub took in the group. "Don't be lingering with all your gabbing. I need Kate back to work. And, Nate, I know she'll need your help too, so get moving."

"Yes, sir," Nate said. "We're just finishing up here."

"Are you involved in her research?" Ian asked Nate.

"Yes," Nate said, flashing a smile. "Lucky for me, Kate allowed me to join her project. I'm finishing up my PhD, and it's an honor to work with her."

Kate beamed. "Thank you. That's very nice of you to say."

"I'm not being nice," Nate said, gathering Kate's lunch tray and assorted wrappers for her. "It's the truth." He held up her half-full bottled water. "You want to save this?"

"Sure." Kate took the bottled water. Nate left the table, taking care of Kate's trash for her. Kate stood and took a drink. Well, wasn't that attentive and gentlemanly? And he must do it often or Kate wouldn't be casually drinking water like it was business as usual.

"Is Nate going with you to Geneva?" Ian asked.

"Probably," Kate said. "I'm allowed to bring a research assistant. Actually a lot of the guys want to go for a chance to work at the Large Hadron Collider. It makes the most sense to bring him, though, since he's familiar with my research."

Nate appeared at Kate's side. "Very familiar. Ready to head back?"

Kate nodded and set off with the men in tow. They walked on either side of her, like bees hovering around their queen. Ian had to wedge himself in between Kate and Nate.

"So did you tell your friends the good news?" Ian asked.

"What good news?" Nate asked, stepping a pace ahead of Ian and turning to look directly at Kate.

"Ian and I are engaged," Kate said flatly. The flat tone stung, though she probably just didn't want to show her enthusiasm in front of her fellow physicists.

"Where's your ring?" Nate asked, grabbing Kate's bare hand and holding it up. He squinted. "Must be a tiny diamond because I don't see it."

Kate snatched her hand back. "You know I don't wear jewelry. Besides, I proposed to Ian, so he'll be the one wearing a ring."

"You proposed to him?" Nate exclaimed.

Kate flushed pink.

"I was happy to accept," Ian put in.

"So no ring for you?" Nate asked Kate. "That sucks."

"It doesn't suck at all!" Kate exclaimed. "I'll get him a ring after the trial run."

Ian winced. "Kate," he started.

Kate's hands fluttered in the air. "Forget I said that. That was just between the two of us. Onward." She strode quickly toward the exit, and the men hurried to keep up.

"Trial run?" Nate asked. "Sounds like the groom has cold feet."

"I don't have cold feet," Ian assured Kate and everyone else.

Kate stopped walking abruptly and looked up at Ian in surprise. "You don't?"

Nate chortled with glee. "That's not what you want in a groom. Bum-bum-de-*doomed*!" He made a big slap-down gesture. Ian gritted his teeth.

All the guys laughed.

Kate frowned and turned to Nate. "Be nice to my boyfriend or you can find another research project."

"I'm sorry," Nate said, immediately contrite. "I was out of line."

"It's okay," Kate said.

Nate dropped to his knees in front of Kate. "Please forgive me, future Nobel Prize-winning physicist!" he exclaimed in a voice full of mischief and humor.

The group and several nearby tables full of people watched them with interest. Ian's hands were in fists.

Kate blushed. "Nate, get up. It's okay."

Ian shoved Nate by the shoulder, and he tipped sideways but managed not to land on his ass.

Nate leaped to his feet and shoved Ian. "You want a go at me?" And that playful voice was gone.

"Nate!" Kate exclaimed.

Ian shoved Nate. "You bet I do. Suck-up."

Colt and Ty stepped between them. "Chill," Colt said.

"Yeah, chill," Ty said.

"This is just like the gorillas," Kate muttered before striding toward the door.

The men followed in her wake.

Ian strode ahead to walk by her side. Where he fucking belonged. Losers.

**8**

Kate finished up her fellowship application on Wednesday at five p.m. A little later than she'd hoped but still by the deadline. She'd worked late in her office on Monday and Tuesday night and had promised Ian she'd be back at her apartment tonight in time for them to share dinner. The application had taken her longer than she'd first thought because she had to mess around with the data in spreadsheets and make it pretty with a bunch of different color-coded and labeled graphs. Usually she preferred to run quick graphs of the data and just focus on the statistical analysis, looking for patterns and visualizing what it all meant in her mind.

Nate walked with her to deliver it to Dr. Weintraub, in case he had any questions or wanted anything additional from them. Nate would stay late for whatever extra work was needed. "You still coming to trivia night at O'Donoghue's tomorrow?" he asked.

"Of course! We're undefeated. I wouldn't miss it."

Nate flashed a smile, and Kate quickly looked away. Something about Nate's smile always took her a little by surprise. Like he suddenly transformed from a fellow physicist to a hottie. It was unsettling.

"Maybe your boyfriend could be on Mike's team," Nate said.

Usually she and Nate paired up, Colt and Ty paired up, and Mike just watched and drank beer. Mike had once joined Colt and Ty, but they argued so much that they pushed Mike out. Nate wouldn't consider a team of three. He said having Kate on his team was already an unfair advantage to all the other teams. He was so funny. Mike claimed not to care about trivia, but she'd noticed how closely he paid attention, so she tried once to recruit another player from the bar. The woman took one look at Mike with his greasy hair and stained clothes and passed. Kate used to be just like Mike before her stylish sister helped her clean up a bit with the fashion sense. Not that she was a fashionista, but she was light-years ahead of Mike.

"That sounds like an excellent idea," Kate said. "Mike needs a partner, and I'm sure Ian will also do quite well at trivia."

"So you and Ian are pretty serious?"

"Yes."

"So why the trial run?"

"It's a smart idea to treat marriage as scientifically as the rest of my life. There's a wealth of literature on marriage outcomes and factors that lead to long-term unions. Not only that, I've discovered a wide range of compatibility quizzes."

Nate stopped walking a short distance from Dr. Weintraub's door. "You know, it might not be my place to say, but…"

"What?"

He stepped into her personal space bubble, and she breathed in his intoxicating spicy cologne. She was very susceptible to cologne. She hugged her packet of papers to her chest and took a careful step back.

Nate leaned close anyway. "I have to wonder, if you need a trial run and quizzes, if he's really the right one for you."

Kate breathed through her mouth to avoid becoming susceptible to his cologne. "That's what the science will prove or disprove."

"Kate," he said gently, "maybe you're too close to see it,

but he's not like you. Not like us. He doesn't get science, doesn't live and breathe it like we do."

"Differentiation is important in a relationship," she replied.

Nate tsked. "Opposites attract is a myth. You want someone like you for a lifetime commitment."

She stared at him, an uneasy feeling swirling through her. "What are you trying to say?"

He stepped back and put his hands up with a boyish grin. "Nothing."

"That's not true. I definitely sensed some kind of subtext. You should know I don't do subtext. Just spell it out for me."

He leaned against the wall, crossing his ankles. "Relationships should be easy when they're right. If you need science to prove someone's right for you, maybe you've already got your answer."

She gasped. "You're saying Ian's not right for me?"

He lifted one shoulder. "Science will tell you that answer. Not me."

"He's the most right thing in my life," she snapped. "And I don't like all this weird talk from you. Stick to physics."

She stalked past him and into Dr. Weintraub's office. "Here," she said, shoving the packet of papers at him.

"Everything all right?" Dr. Weintraub asked.

"Yes," she snapped.

Nate stepped into the office. "Everything should be in order. Let me know if you need anything else."

Dr. Weintraub looked curiously from Kate to Nate. Omigod, their names rhymed. She'd never noticed that before. How cutesy. She had to get out of here. Fast.

"Can you stay, Nate?" she asked. "I promised Ian I'd meet him for dinner."

"Of course," Nate said, taking a seat while Dr. Weintraub looked through the paperwork.

"Text me if you need anything further from me and I'll return right away," Kate said.

"I'm sure that won't be necessary," Dr. Weintraub said,

thumbing through the color-coded graphs. "Enjoy your dinner."

Kate drove home, anxious to see Ian again. She parked in the lot behind the three-story brick building that served as graduate housing with several furnished apartments. (The university let postdocs stay there too.) She picked up speed once inside the building, raced up the stairs, and burst into her apartment. It struck her that Ian was exactly as she'd left him this morning, lounging on the brown sofa, watching the small TV on its stand in the living room.

"You didn't cook dinner," she blurted. Where had that come from?

He sat up. "We'll go out."

She dropped her purse and coat, annoyed for some reason. "So you just lounge around all day and expect me to cook dinner when I get home?"

His brows shot up. "I said we'd go out."

She wrung her hands together. "Relationships should pass the test of science. Right?"

He crossed to her, pulled her hands apart, and wrapped his arms around her. She rested her head against his chest, listening to his steady heartbeat.

"He made me doubt," she mumbled.

He pulled back and looked at her. "Who made you doubt?"

"Nate. He said that we shouldn't need an experiment or a trial run. We should just know if it's right."

Ian clenched his jaw. "As much as I don't want to agree with that guy, it's true you just know if it's right."

"But I don't know!" she cried.

"I know."

"Why don't I know?"

He hugged her tight. "Because I made you doubt. I'm sorry, Kate. I know it'll get easier. I've never been engaged before." He pulled back and met her eyes. "You remember Morgan gave me that ultimatum? She said marry her or she'd walk." Morgan was Ian's last girlfriend. They'd been together for three years.

"And you walked," she whispered.

He dipped his head. "Maybe since it wasn't my idea this time either, I got kind of a trapped feeling, like it was another ultimatum. I mean 'no' wasn't really an acceptable answer."

She pulled out of his arms, alarmed. "Of course it was! I want you to be honest. You should never say yes when you mean no."

He crossed his arms. "Really? Honestly? You would've been fine with me saying no? Then we'd go right back to normal?"

She thought about that, remembering kneeling in her hydrogen costume that she'd had made special for the biggest surprise she could think of. She would've been devastated. Mortified. Ready to flee the scene.

"I guess it was a dumb surprise," she murmured.

He grabbed her hand and tugged her close. "It was a surprise. That's all. Not dumb."

"Will you still do the experiment with me? I've put a lot of thought into it. A lot of research." And, despite his reassurances, she needed to know conclusively, scientifically, that things would work out.

He lifted her hand and kissed the back of it. Warmth spread through her. "If you want to do it, we'll do it."

Her throat was tight, making it difficult to speak. "And what if the outcome is negative?"

"I'll still love you just as much. Who else would take their relationship so seriously that they'd develop rigorous scientific testing? It's thoughtful, that's what it is." He cupped her face in his warm hands. "You, with this brilliant mind, gifted your valuable brain power on *us*. That shows me, more than anything, how much you care."

"Oh, Ian!" She threw her arms around his neck, so grateful for the way he really got her. She'd almost doubted them. Stupid Nate putting stupid doubts in her head. "I do care! So, so much! You're the best, most important person in my life." She kissed him. "I love you."

He scooped her up, cradled in his arms, and she snuggled into his chest. "I love you too, sweetheart."

Then he carried her into the bedroom and showed her how much he loved her.

A long while later, lying on her belly, too limp to even roll over, Kate found herself thinking of their scientifically based trial run. She really wished she could just let it go and not worry. She knew Ian loved her. Believed it with her whole heart. Yet she still doubted he was over his cold feet. She was sure he'd just said that he was over it to spite Nate.

Some part of her worried Ian would leave her. At the altar or before that, when the trapped feeling got too much for him. After all, he'd never lived with her before. She knew she was…quirky, and he'd been mostly understanding of her quirks, but he'd never had to live with them twenty-four seven. There was no way around it. They had to go through with the experiment and discover for themselves if they really had what it took to go the distance.

Ian fully acknowledged Kate was a beautiful, sexy, brilliant woman. He just didn't like having all these other guys acknowledging it too. Kate brought him along to trivia night at O'Donoghue's with her adoring guy crew. They sat at a large table not too far from where the quizmaster would ask the questions. The bar was near campus and full of legal-age students and a handful of professors. Nate went straight to the bar.

Ian slipped an arm around Kate. "What do you want to drink?" He kinda hoped she'd say iced tea. He wasn't keen on thinking of Kate drinking beer and being lusty around these guys. He had to wonder if she had been when he wasn't around to witness it.

Kate gestured to the bar. "Nate's got it."

He glanced over to where Nate was apparently ordering for her.

Ian hightailed it to the bar. "Hey, Nate, whatcha getting?"

"Two beers, my friend," Nate said.

The bartender arrived; Nate paid and left a hefty tip

before heading back to the table. So Nate was a big spender. He was a grad student (they typically had little money), so he must come from money. Another strike against him, Ian thought grimly.

Ian ordered a beer for himself, and by the time he got back to the table, taking a seat next to Kate, everyone had paired up. Nate sat on Kate's other side.

"Ian, you're with Mike," Kate said.

"Kate and I are always a team," Nate said smugly. "Undefeated." He lifted a fist and Kate gave him a fist bump.

"Actually, Kate, I want to be with you," Ian said. The hell with subtle. She needed a clear message, and he was happy to send it.

Nate piped up. "We can't break our streak. Two more levels and we'll be the champs. We'll get the O'Donoghue Cup and a thousand dollars." He jerked a thumb over to where a large trophy stood in a place of honor at the quizmaster's table.

Sorry. This was about much more than a trophy and prize money, and Ian had to put his foot down. He wouldn't share Kate, and especially not with the guy who openly adored her and who filled her head with doubts about Ian and Kate's relationship. Nope. Not gonna happen.

"Kate," Ian said simply. He really didn't want to get into it again with Nate, but the man was a little too smug about his place with Kate, and Ian seriously wanted to punch him.

Kate pushed her hair behind her ears. "What?"

"Tell him you want to be on my team," Ian said. Direct, honest, to the point. She'd appreciate that given that was how she operated.

Kate looked from him to Nate, seeming torn.

"It really shouldn't be that tough of a decision," Ian said.

"Easiest decision in the world," Nate said. "Go with a winner." He pumped his fists in the air. "Victory!"

"No one wants to play with shlubby old Mike," Mike said from the far end of the table. "Whatever."

"Sorry, man," Colt said to Mike. "You just didn't gel with

us. Besides, Ty and I have a history in this game. Last year we came in second place."

"Mike, don't be sad!" Kate exclaimed. "I'll be on your team."

Mike grinned. "Really? Great!"

Kate stood.

"Kate!" Ian and Nate said at the same time.

"Ian will take my place on the team," she said, gesturing Ian over to Nate. "And, guys, don't go gorilla on me." She grabbed her beer and headed for the far end of the table away from both of them.

Nate shot Ian a dark look. "We won't win without Kate."

"Hey, I'm a good player," Ian said. "You could still win the big trophy to make up for your little—"

"Shut up," Nate snapped.

"Everything okay down there?" Kate asked from the other end of the table.

"Everything's great!" Ian said. "We're definitely going to lose without you."

"Oh, Ian! You're so funny!" She giggled and drank some beer.

He grinned, leaned back and clasped his hands behind his head. Someone was getting lucky tonight. And it wasn't Nate.

A short while later, the trivia game began. The quizmaster announced the category and then the question. They had sixty seconds to enter an answer on an app on their cell phone. The app temporarily disabled Internet access to prevent cheating. First question was on sports.

"You know sports?" Nate asked Ian.

"Yeah," Ian said, though he only knew baseball.

"Okay," Nate said, "you take sports. I'll take everything else."

"What do you do when sports comes up with Kate?" Ian asked.

"We guess," Nate said.

"Mike knows sports!" Kate called to them with a big smile. She turned to Mike. "We are *so* going to win!"

Mike grinned.

"Who scored the first points in Super Bowl history?" the quizmaster asked. "Sixty seconds."

Nate looked to Ian anxiously.

"Reggie Jackson," Ian replied just to mess with him. That was a former Yankees baseball player.

Nate typed it in eagerly. Ian bit back a smile. This could be fun.

Next question, also sports: What basketball player played the most seasons in the NBA?

Nate looked to Ian.

"Terry Bradshaw," Ian answered with a straight face. That was a former football quarterback.

Nate dutifully typed it in. Every time Nate asked him a question, Ian fed him the wrong answer. Sure, it was juvenile, but the guy deserved it. And every time Nate thought he knew the answer, Ian would peek over his shoulder and introduce some doubt. "Are you sure about that answer?"

"Yes, yes, I'm sure," Nate would say.

"Hmm…" Ian replied mysteriously.

Then Nate would, all on his own, come up with some possible scenario where it could be a different answer. Of course, Ian readily agreed with the amended incorrect answer. It was just too easy. The hardest part was doing it all with a straight face.

An hour later, the quizmaster ran the results through the computer and declared Kate and Mike the winners.

"Yes!" Mike shouted.

Kate bounced in her seat, grinning from ear-to-ear. "We did it!"

They high-fived with first one hand, then the other, and then both.

Nate scowled.

"Welp," Ian said, "good game. Now I've gotta collect my lusty woman."

Nate huffed. "I can't believe we did so poorly."

Ian tried really hard not to laugh. "Them's the breaks."

"I thought you knew sports," Nate said.

Ian finished his beer and stood. "I know more than you."

Nate started typing on his cell phone, probably looking up the answers now that he had an Internet connection. Time to go.

He headed to the other end of the table, where Kate was, in her direct honest way, giving Mike advice on women.

"You're really a wonderful partner," she was saying. "There's no reason why any woman in this bar wouldn't like to join you."

Mike blushed and stared at the table. "Thanks, Kate," he mumbled.

"There's two things you need to do before you can attract a partner," Kate went on matter-of-factly. Mike's head snapped up. "You must wash your hair."

"I do wash my hair," Mike protested.

It really didn't look like it. The greasy strands hung lank and too long.

"Then you must up the frequency," Kate said.

"More than once a week?" Mike asked.

"Yes, I would suggest an every-other-day schedule," Kate said. "Alternatively, you could get a buzz cut and go for every three days."

"Oh-kay," Mike said slowly. "If you really think it would help."

"A woman gives you woman advice," Ian put in. "That's gold."

Mike nodded and shoved a hank of hair out of his eyes.

Kate went on. "And while I understand the attachment to old comfortable T-shirts, some of mine are seven years old—"

"This is ten years old," Mike said proudly, holding out the shirt by the hem that was stained in multiple places with what looked like pizza sauce.

"You need shirts with no stains," Kate said. "I'll email you a link to an online store where you can stock up on multiple colors for a very reasonable price."

"But new T-shirts aren't broken in," Mike said.

Kate cocked her head. "Would you like to attract a mate? I sensed despair and desperation in your plea that no one ever wanted to partner with shlubby Mike."

Ian bit back a smile. Kate kept surprising him. She was reading between the lines and acting accordingly. Maybe he could mess with her a little more and she'd get the joke.

Mike blushed. "I'm not desperate or whatever."

"When was the last time you were with a woman?" Kate asked. *Ooh! Nut cruncher.* Poor Mike.

When Mike didn't answer, Ian worked on looking like it was all business as usual. "No judgment here," Ian said.

"It's been a while," Mike admitted.

Kate grabbed her coat and purse. "Okay. Next month at trivia night, I want to see you with clean hair and a clean shirt, and then we'll approach a nice woman and invite her to be your partner. I will vouch for your skill and for your general awesomeness."

Mike grinned. "You're on."

Kate waved to the group. "Bye, all! See you tomorrow."

"Bye, Kate!" the men chorused.

"Next time you're on my team!" Nate called.

"Oh, Nate!" Kate laughed and shook her head. "See you tomorrow!" She headed for the door. "He's so ridiculous," she whispered to Ian. "He's better at trivia than I am."

Ian dropped an arm over her shoulders, pulled her close, and kissed her cheek. "You're amazing."

She turned to him, eyes wide. "Why would you say that?"

He held the door open for her. "You really helped Mike out in a way that probably no one else could. Very direct and honest."

Her brows scrunched together. "I don't know how to be any other way."

He joined her outside and took her hand. "And that's to Mike's benefit."

She smiled up at him. "That's to everyone's benefit. Everyone should be honest."

He ran his thumb across the underside of her wrist. "How'd that beer make you feel?"

"Lusty. You're up, Furnukle."

He threw back his head and laughed. "I love you, Kate."

"I love you too. You up for it?"

He grabbed her and nuzzled into her neck, breathing in her fresh soap and fruity grapefruit scent from her shampoo. "Always for you." Her cheek touched his, and he realized she was smiling.

She pulled back and met his eyes. "Thanks for not making a big deal about joining Nate's team. I just thought Mike really wanted to play for once."

"No problem. It was fun."

"Really? I thought you didn't like him."

He cocked a brow. "And why wouldn't I like him?"

"I don't know. Because he's coming with me to Geneva, because he adores me, because he said you and I shouldn't need a trial run."

"Well, I think he's swell," he replied in his best oh-golly sarcastic voice.

She giggled and started walking again. "I'm anxious to do our trial run. Have you ever had a roommate?"

"Not in a long time. Since grad school. I'm sure you'll be the best roommate I ever had."

"How do you know?"

He grinned. "Because you'll be my first roommate with benefits."

"Should we devise a schedule for our living arrangement?"

"You'd like that, wouldn't you?"

She nodded vigorously.

"Benefits every night and every morning."

"You don't think you'll get tired? I mean, that's great for a vacation, but do you really have the stamina for it?"

He stopped walking and mimed plunging a knife through his heart. "You wound me."

"Not that you're old or anything."

"I have the stamina. Geez, Kate, I'm only twenty-eight. I'll slow down when I'm dead."

She gave him an impish smile. "I'm just saying there's a reason they have those little blue pills."

He yanked her flush against him, kissing her long and deep, letting things heat up right there on the sidewalk. She let out a needy moan, wrapped her arms around his neck, and, a moment later, lifted her leg to wrap around his. He loved when she climbed his body. It meant she wanted him bad.

He shifted to speak in a low voice near her ear. "Let's go. I've got something to prove now."

"I hope you'll hit a ten."

"I always hit a ten." He stopped, taking in her mischievous smile. "You!"

She stopped smiling. "What?"

"You've been teasing me with that ten stuff. I've always been a ten. You're just egging me on."

She put a hand on her hip, all sassy. "What if I am?"

He grabbed her and tickled her. She laughed like crazy and wiggled away from him. "I can't believe you!" he exclaimed. "You know how hard I work *every time* to measure up?"

She threw her arms around him, went up on tiptoe, and whispered in his ear, "You're the inspiration for the rating system. You're the perfect ten, from the very first time, which no one else has ever measured up to."

He got choked up. He was her first, and she'd never had better after him. *He* set the bar. That meant something to him. "Kate," he managed, his voice gruff with emotion.

"Come on," she said, leading him back toward her apartment. "I can't wait for your next ten. And no slacking!"

He swatted her bottom, and she yelped. "You'll be eating those words."

**9**

———

**May in Boston…**

*The ordeal begins.* Ian had no sooner helped Kate move all her luggage into his one-bedroom apartment than she settled on the living room sofa, opened her laptop, and announced, "I have the experiment and all relevant data points worked out."

It was Sunday afternoon, and for some crazy reason he'd thought maybe she'd want to go out. Or, even better, go straight to bed. Not start the science stuff right away. They had all month. Spring in Boston was glorious—seventy degrees with a light breeze, blue skies, all the flowering trees in bloom. It was a short walk to the beautiful Boston Common from his apartment. He really should've known better. But over the last month and a half when they'd been long distance, she hadn't mentioned the experiment once. He'd kinda sorta hoped—

"I've prepared everything we need," Kate went on seriously. She gave him a quick glance. "Please take a seat." Her tone was formal, which meant she was worked up about this experiment. She gestured in a jerky, stiff motion to the far end of the sofa away from her.

He crossed to the sofa and tried to sit next to her. She

shoved his butt. "You can't be too close. You know how you trip my circuit. I need all my mental power."

He turned, slid his hand into her hair, and leaned down to her. Her eyes drifted closed, and he brushed his lips over hers. "That can wait. I missed you."

She leaned back and then replied in her direct way, "We'll make love as soon as we've completed part one of the experiment."

He got a really bad feeling. "How many parts are there?"

"Twelve. Please take a seat so we may begin. The sooner we start, the sooner we can move things to the bedroom."

He stifled a groan and sat at the far end of the sofa.

She pushed her glasses up. "This first part I estimate will take an hour, or more if the discussion topics open up other relevant areas we should explore."

This felt like that high-stakes game of questions she'd put him through on the plane ride to Chicago back in March. He hadn't done so well. "Kate, we don't have to do all that."

Her brows scrunched together. "We don't?"

"Let's just play it by ear. We'll live together for a month and see how it goes."

She scowled. "But I've prepared so much. Not only the twelve-part experimental investigation, but also a five-part relationship compatibility test compiling the best of the Internet's relationship questions and the most common reasons for divorce."

He suppressed a shudder. Then he reached over and shut the laptop. "Just ask me whatever it is you're concerned about."

She rattled off her concerns in a barrage of questions. "How do you see our future? Where will we live? Whose career will take precedence? Will we have children? Who will be the caretaker? Who will keep up with domestic responsibilities? How will we handle money decisions?"

He felt light-headed. "Whoa."

"I want a tenured position at a university. Would you move to where that is?"

He cleared his throat. "Or alternatively—"

"We have a long-distance marriage."

He was getting a headache. This was their argument from a few months ago. "No long distance once we're married," he said firmly. "We need to explore all the options and find a compromise."

"And if there is no room for compromise? Who gets priority? The one with the higher salary? Some other objective measure of importance?"

He thought about that. How did you decide job priority in a fair way? He'd never considered it before. "We need more information," he finally said. "Let's wait to hear on your fellowship application."

"Fine. I should hear by May twenty-sixth at the latest."

"Then we'll go back to that one."

She nodded once. "Next, will we have children?"

He relaxed a little. "Yes, two would work, but no rush."

"That works for me too." She met his eyes in a direct gaze. "And let me stop right here to say not only do I look forward to making those children with you, but I consider you the ideal father."

His chest puffed with pride. "Thank you."

She pushed her glasses up. "No need to thank me, it's simply a fact. You have great genes both in physical attractiveness and intelligence with a pleasing easygoing temperament."

He was beginning to feel like a breeding stallion. Maybe she'd like to check his teeth next. He bit back a sarcastic remark and merely said, "Uh-huh."

"And you come from a loving family with a father who set a good example both as a provider and a caretaker."

"Yes," he managed over the lump in his throat. He still missed his dad, a brilliant mechanical engineer and a loving dad with a playful sense of humor. He'd died six years ago from a heart attack. Kate had never met his dad, but she knew about him from his family's stories.

"So we need to decide," Kate said, "if we both have day jobs, who will be our children's caretaker. Babysitter? Daycare?"

"I thought you'd take time off." His own mom had stayed home to raise him and his two older brothers.

"I thought you'd take time off," she fired back.

He jolted. He'd never considered that. "Me?"

"Why not? Of the two of us, you're more nurturing. I certainly didn't have that example in my family."

"But I'm the guy." He didn't know any guy who did that, not his own dad, not his friends, not even his older brother Barry, who adored his daughter.

Kate's eyes flashed. "You're *the guy* in the twenty-first century."

"Ouch."

"Yes, ouch. Should we move on to money?"

He swallowed. "I guess."

"Joint account?"

"Sure."

"Who decides what to spend it on and how much to save?"

"We both do," he answered confidently.

She opened the laptop and clicked a few times. Then she turned the screen toward him. "Here's a spreadsheet I've made of estimated future earnings, timing of children, factoring in time off for pregnancies and postpartum care." She met his eyes. "I've created three scenarios for zero, one, or two children. I don't think it's wise to let the children outnumber the adults so..." She turned back to her spreadsheet and clicked. "Here's what I estimate we'll have to earn to accommodate a mortgage, two kids, college savings, and future retirement."

He felt light-headed again.

"Ian, are you okay?"

He saw spots. Suddenly dizzy, he put his head between his knees.

A moment later, Kate knelt at his side and rubbed his back. "I can see you're not ready for a committed future with me."

He spoke from between his legs. "I thought we'd be talking about who does the laundry."

"We'll discuss that after we've worked out our financial future for our mutual life expectancy."

"This is so serious," he croaked.

"Life is serious."

He lifted his head, rested his elbows on his knees, and focused on breathing until the light-headed feeling passed. "What if we just said whatever happens happens?"

"Chaos."

"Fun."

"I'm uncomfortable with this scenario."

His lips twitched. "I'll ease you into it."

"Ian, I'm pregnant."

He passed out.

Kate stared down at an unconscious Ian flopped sideways on the sofa. She sighed. If he'd just gone along with her experiment, she could've eased him into the tough questions. She went to the kitchen, filled a cup with a small amount of cold water, grabbed a paper towel, and returned to Mr. Cold Feet.

She threw the water in his face.

He sputtered and shook his head. "What happened?"

She handed him the paper towel to dry off. "That was a test. I'm not pregnant, and you're clearly not ready for a permanent commitment."

He wiped his face with the towel and tossed it aside. "A test?" he asked with an edge to his voice.

She eased back a step, but he snagged her by the hips. "Ian!"

He pulled her on top of him. "A test? Do not *test* me, Kate!" He swatted her bottom lightly, and she giggled. "Let's test you, shall we?"

She met his warm brown eyes. "Please do."

"Aww, Kate, I love you."

"I love you too," she said, her whole body filling with warmth at the words that she meant with all her heart. Or maybe that was Ian's body heating her up.

He pushed a lock of hair over her ear. "Let's just keep doing what we're doing. I'll even work from home part-time this month to maximize our time together. Isn't living together the best way to see if we're compatible?"

"I don't know. I fear you passing out is a red flag that I can't ignore."

He grimaced. "I'll admit I'm not ready *right now* for kids and a mortgage, but that doesn't mean I'm not ready to be engaged. One step at a time."

She considered that. Perhaps she had jumped ahead. She enjoyed having her future mapped out, but maybe Ian needed a looser framework. Still, she'd prepared so much for her experiment, she hated to see all that work go to waste.

"What about my spreadsheet on our financial future?" she asked.

"Table it until we have more data."

"And my compatibility quizzes?"

"I'll take *one*."

She beamed and kissed him. "Thank you."

He ran his hands under her T-shirt and stroked the bare skin of her back. Warm tingles radiated everywhere he touched her. She told herself to focus before the short circuit shut down her brain completely.

"Can we still do my twelve-part experiment?" she asked urgently. Her bra sprang open. She hurried to add, "I think it's solidly constructed with potentially useful results."

"Can we condense it a bit?" he asked. His hands stroked up her sides, pushing her bra up out of the way, and her sharp focus softened along with her body.

"How?" she breathed.

"One experiment topic a day?" he suggested, brushing along the sides of her breasts. A rush of shivery pleasure went through her.

"Yes," she said on a sigh. "Twelve days in a row. Knock it out."

His hand slid down her spine to her ass, cupping her between the legs. His fingers curled in, pressing at her entrance through her jeans. A rush of dampness and pleasure surged between her legs. Somehow he always hit the right spots even through her clothes. Short circuit tripped, she melted against him.

His other hand slid into her hair, tilting her head up. "It's really important we keep up the experimental testing in the bedroom," he said with a wicked smile.

"I'm open to anything and everything with you," she said eagerly.

His gaze turned hot, his fingers tightening in her hair before his mouth claimed hers. Her brain shut down as wanton need took over. He kissed her breathless, his hands all over her; then he sat up, taking her with him, and yanked her shirt over her head. Her bra went flying. And then she was airborne, Ian carrying her to the bedroom for the first of many brilliant experimental explorations.

Her boyfriend was a freaking genius.

His girlfriend was a freaking genius.

He knew this, yet he hadn't thought about what that meant for him actually living with her. It had only been a week and, hell, she was hard to live with. His apartment was a disaster area. Not like he was Mr. Neat, but…she left Post-its with equations all over the place, he even found one on the eggs, and the butter had a weird symbol carved into it. The small bathroom mirror was regularly covered in lipsticked equations, making it impossible for him to get a good look at himself when shaving. Worse, and grosser, the shower wall was covered with odd scattered dots of his shaving cream. He wasn't allowed to touch any of this stuff, as he'd discovered when he'd tried to rinse off the shower wall after three days of looking at weird pointy hard dots of shaving cream.

"Ian! That was an important randomized scatter graph! I haven't completed the math on it yet. I have to study it during my showers."

"Could we take a picture of it before it gets moldy and gross?"

"I often have breakthroughs in the shower. I need them there."

He told himself she was a brilliant physicist and sometimes brilliant people had little quirks. But the following Monday that little quirk seemed more like a pathological deal-breaker. It was early morning, he was in a rush, as usual, but today was especially important because he had several job applicants to interview at the lab and needed to look like a competent boss. Problem was when he opened the medicine cabinet above the sink, no shaving cream. He immediately hunted the pathological equation-writer down. (Would it kill her to use pen and paper?)

He found Kate in the living room on her laptop, already showered and dressed.

"Where's my shaving cream?" he demanded. He hadn't shaved all weekend, and now he was at that scruffy stage between stubble and full-on beard. Not work appropriate.

She blinked slowly and stared at him, uncomprehending. He'd learned when she was immersed in equations, it took a few moments for her to return to the real world.

"I can't find my shaving cream," he said. "Do you have it?"

She looked dreamily off in the distance.

"Kate!"

She snapped her head back to him. "Oh. I ran out of lipstick."

He marched back to the bathroom, ripped the shower curtain back, and saw the evidence. She must've finished the can, writing in symbols and numbers only Kate understood, on all three walls of the shower from top to bottom. He did some deep breathing. He couldn't be late. His first interview appointment was at eight. He had exactly forty-five minutes to shave, shower, dress, and catch the train. He didn't have time to run out to the store, and shaving with soap always left him with a zillion tiny cuts. He marched back to the living room, where Kate had returned to whatever equations were fascinating her.

"Kate!"

Her head snapped up, and she blinked at him. Her gaze trailed down his bare chest to his boxer briefs, where she remained riveted. His traitorous cock perked up involuntarily. Dammit. This was not the time.

"This is important," he said through his teeth. "I have to interview new hires today."

She slowly raised her gaze and met his eyes. "You'd better get ready, then."

"I need to shave, and there's no more shaving cream."

She put her laptop down. "I'll go to the store."

"There's no time!" Besides, every time Kate ran an errand, she ended up walking for blocks and blocks, thinking. Half the time she forgot what she'd left the house for.

"I'm sorry," she said. "I didn't know the can was so close to empty."

"It wasn't close to empty until you sprayed it all over three walls!"

She held up a finger. "Just a minute. I'll ask my cell phone." She went for her phone.

Ian started pacing. "Great. Ask your cell phone. Sure, it has *all* the answers."

Kate nodded, completely missing his sarcasm. She pressed the button on her cell and spoke slowly and clearly. "What are alternatives to shaving cream?"

The phone replied back in a female robot voice. "Here are places on the web with alternatives to shaving cream."

Ian ground his teeth.

Kate tapped a few times and rattled off several options, none of which he had. "Hand lotion, almond oil, apricot oil—"

"I don't have any of that shit! Forget it! I'll look like a slob."

"Soap!" she said triumphantly. "You definitely have soap."

"It doesn't work as well. I'll end up with bloody cuts."

She looked down at her cell again. "Peanut butter."

"Yeah. I'd love to smell like peanut butter all day." He let out a breath. "Fine, I'll use soap. Who cares if I show up to work bleeding?"

"I could shave for you."

"No, thanks." She'd probably shave a mathematical symbol onto his face while she dreamed of equations. He'd be pi man.

He huffed and marched back to the bathroom, did his best with the soap, and emerged with five scraps of toilet paper stuck to his neck and jaw to stop the bleeding. Then he took a quick shower and dressed in his nicest business casual outfit. He returned to the living room. "How do I look?"

She lifted her head from her laptop and murmured, "Great. Have fun."

He wasn't sure she'd even looked at him. Or that she understood interviewing new hires wasn't "fun." All she saw were freaking equations. "Bye."

"Bye, pookie!" she called.

He clenched his jaw and kept walking toward the door. Apparently the marriage literature said couples with cute nicknames for each other had higher marital satisfaction. He couldn't even…

"I'll be here when you get back," she said, which was kind of sweet. "Unless I take a walk," she added.

"Bye," he said tersely and marched out the door.

When he returned home, after what turned out to be not such a bad day after all, Kate met him at the door, took his hand and led him back toward the bedroom. His day just got a whole lot better. But at the last second, she turned him toward the bathroom and flung open the door.

"Ta-dah!" she exclaimed. "I've taken care of the problem."

There was a pyramid of shaving cream cans taking up all the open space. Must've been at least a hundred cans. Guess he wouldn't be running out anytime soon.

He slowly shook his head, bemused. He turned to find her eagerly waiting for his response. "You took care of the problem all right."

She beamed. "We'll never have that fight again."

Only Kate. Life with her would never be boring. That was

for sure. Then a thought occurred to him. "What do you use at your place when you have inspiration in the shower?"

"I have a waterproof notebook and pen."

"Order a hundred of those for here."

"A hundred? That seems like a lot."

He gestured to the hundred shaving cream cans.

"That's a hundred and five. I had to go to six stores." At his hard look, she quickly amended. "Great idea."

He pulled her close and kissed the top of her head. "Okay, Kate. Problem solved."

"One week successfully completed," she chirped. "Three more to go."

"Piece of cake," he said and really tried to mean it.

## 10

Kate sat on the living room sofa, typing furiously on her laptop while Ian showered. *Week two of the captivity experiment. Male and female chimps remain in love with frequent rigorous copulation (daily). Female has adapted to new surroundings, making use of resources at hand. Male shows signs of territoriality. Note: may be related to perceived lack of resources. Female working on determining which resources must be kept in plentiful supply. Shaving cream at the top of the list.*

She'd been forced to supplement her condensed experiment with detailed observations due to the male's noncompliance with all aspects of the experiment. It was important as a scientist that she maintain some objective distance, as she'd told Ian, so she framed her observations as if she were watching two chimps she'd never met before. She considered for a moment if there were any other solutions to the territoriality problem.

She typed again. *Alternative solution—his and hers labels on perceived high-value items.*

"Kate!"

Kate reluctantly lifted her gaze from the laptop and observed the male chimp pacing in a display of frustration, tension, and possible alpha dominance (he was naked except for a towel around his waist and impressive in his masculinity—tall, broad-shouldered, defined biceps, dark inverted triangle of chest hair leading to his usual bulge).

"Eyes up here!" he demanded.

She blinked, met his eyes, and waited for a clearer message. He was fresh from the shower. That usually relaxed him. So why the hostile stance? Jaw tight, hands on hips, feet wide apart.

She looked off in the distance, pondering this puzzle. The shower walls were clean now. She'd scrubbed them down last night when she'd finally hit upon the equation she needed to make the scatter graph fit with her theory. Hmm...there certainly wasn't any lack of resources in the bathroom. She was an early riser and took inventory before her own shower this morning of anything that he might perceive to be of high value. Sure, she was out of lipstick, but that shouldn't be a territorial thing for him.

"Kate!"

Her gaze snapped to his. "What?"

"Why do I have zero boxer briefs?" the male chimp inquired in a hostile tone. Ah. Possible wardrobe malfunction. She knew both the solution and the cause.

She quickly started typing in her observation. The laptop snapped closed suddenly. She looked up to find the male, nostrils flaring, glaring down at her. She stood, preferring not to let the alpha display get out of hand. Mmm, he smelled so good.

She went up on tiptoe and kissed his clean-shaven cheek just to breathe him in—fresh clean soap, woodsy with a hint of citrus from his cologne, and pure sexy man.

He grabbed her by the upper arms and looked directly in her eyes. "Kate, what did you do with my boxer briefs?"

"They're gone."

"Gone? Gone?" His voice rose both in pitch and volume on a repeated word. She'd have to make note of that later.

"Yes."

"Why are they gone?"

"To make room for your boxers. Oh! They're still in the bag in the closet—"

"Why did you switch me from boxer briefs to boxers without telling me?" he asked in a surprisingly reasonable tone considering the earlier posturing. He even let go of her arms and gave her a little space.

She pursed her lips, unsure which question was more important. The switch? Or not telling him?

He leaned close and growled in full alpha display, "You have three seconds before all your panties are gone. And I won't be putting anything in their place."

"Ian!"

"Commando, Kate. That's right. One."

"I can't possibly go commando all the time! Some of my clothes might chafe—"

"Two."

"Your panties were in a bunch! You were so tense about your things. I don't even know which things you'll share and which I'm not supposed to touch!" *Territoriality extends to underwear.*

"Is that supposed to be a joke?"

"No," she answered slowly. "It was a metaphor. Your panties, I mean, you're the male, so your *underwear* was in a bunch. You've been so tense with me."

His lips were playing at a smile that made her wary. "I'm the male." For some reason he was focusing on the wrong thing.

"You're supposed to see now that you need to relax about your things," she pointed out helpfully.

His large hand wrapped around the back of her neck and pulled her close. His gaze dropped to her mouth, and her pulse skittered. "You must be the female."

"That's, uh—" she swallowed at the hot look in his eyes "—not the point."

His head dipped low, his words a hot whisper against her ear. "You're tense too." His hand dropped from her neck, both hands coming to rest on her hips.

"If I'm tense, it's only because you—oh!"

The male's dexterity proved impressive. He stripped her shorts and panties in one quick move. She gaped at him. He held her purple panties by one finger. "Say goodbye to these!"

She grabbed for them, but he tossed them toward the foyer; then he grabbed her, lowering them both to the sofa, her under him in a classic dominance play. He slid his fingers into her hair, holding her in his grip as his other hand stroked down her throat. Heat rushed through her.

His eyes locked on hers for one breathless moment. "You taught me a good lesson, Kate. Now I can teach you a good lesson too."

Her heart hammered in anticipation. "But I wasn't tense about my things."

He leaned down and clamped his teeth on the side of her neck, a move that her body knew well from previous animal fuckings. Hot and wet and throbbing, her breath shuddered out.

He released her neck and growled in her ear. "As long as I'm wearing boxers, you'll be wearing nothing."

"I can't—"

His eyes were hot on hers. "You will. And it'll make it so much easier to take you wherever and whenever I want."

She was breathless, hot all over, her breasts tingling, her body aching. "Yes, take me."

"Fuck, Kate, you say all the right things." He lifted off her just long enough to rip the towel off him and took her mouth in a hard claim of possession.

The female surrendered to pleasure immediately.

A few moments later, Ian lifted off her, pulled her up and took off her shirt and bra, which gave her brain time to start working again. She should make her chimps-in-love observations about sex too. That would really round out the picture.

"I have a great idea," she announced.

The male grunted. He lifted her to straddle his lap, where he was now seated on the sofa. "Keep talking," he murmured before arranging her so she was on her knees on either side of his legs. She hung onto his shoulders.

"I want you to be an animal," she said. "Fast, hard, and rough. As primal as a male can be."

"All the right things," he murmured before his mouth closed over her nipple and sucked hard. Electric pleasure shot through her. Her back arched, and his arm banded around her waist, holding her tight. Her nails dug into his shoulders. It felt so unbelievably good, a straight line of pleasure to her throbbing sex. She wanted to grind down on him, but it was impossible with the hold he had on her.

"I'll be an animal too!" she gasped.

He lifted his head. "Yeah, you will."

He moved to her other breast, sucking hard. She held his head to her, the incredible pleasure bringing her up, up, up to that peak she craved. Suddenly he released her, grabbed her ass, and stood with her plastered to his front, arms and legs around him like a chimp. He took her to the wall, her bare back hitting the cold surface, a sharp contrast to the heat at her front.

"Hard," he growled, lifting her and pushing inside just a little, making her crazed.

"Yes. And rough and—"

He thrust deep, her body filling suddenly and fully, the shock and pleasure so intense she gasped. He lifted her again, halfway up, and her body trembled in anticipation. "Let me hear what primal sounds like," he urged and thrust deep again.

She let out a primal cry she'd never known she had in her. He swore and lifted her again, reaching between them to stroke her sweet spot, making her shudder around him. Then she could do nothing but pant as Ian took her like an animal, hard and fast and rough, her primal cries harsh, keening, desperately needy. The pressure was unbearable. She needed her release; her nails scratched down his back. "Fuck," he muttered before his mouth crashed over hers, swallowing her cries as he drove into her over and over. She clung to him, her insides tightening even as he pushed her open with each thrust. Her climax spiked sharp and hot, bringing shock-waves of pleasure. He held her tighter, his hands on her ass, still thrusting through her release. Her breath came in short gasps, her body climbing again, building to another peak.

"I'm close again," she cried.

He grunted, lifted her hips at an angle and thrust deep. She broke violently, taking him with her, his groan loud and long against her neck.

A moment passed with nothing but the sound of their panting. Animal. So animal.

He rested his forehead against hers and finally spoke. "You keep surprising me."

She found herself smiling. "You keep satisfying me."

He laughed. "So are you going to replace the boxer briefs you threw out? I assume you threw them out. You never do anything half-assed." At her quick nod, he went on, "Or do you plan on going commando the rest of the month while I wear old-man boxers?"

"They're not old man," she huffed. "They're a useful metaphorical reminder."

He arched a brow. "I'm liking commando for you more and more. That's a damn useful reminder."

She pursed her lips. "There is no way I'm giving up my underwear. Do you know how hard it is to find panties that are both comfortable and sexy?"

He set her back on the floor and held her by the hips. Her legs felt quivery. How strange. She'd have to make a note of that animal side effect.

"Kate?"

"Huh?"

"I said you owe me fourteen pairs of boxer briefs. Unless you want to go the other way…"

"Fourteen pairs," she muttered. Definitely territorial about underwear. *Male wants exact same amount so no lack of resources.*

He tipped her chin up. "What're you thinking so hard about?"

"I need to get my laptop."

"Why?"

"I need to write some things down. Our activities caused a lot of firing neurons in the aftermath."

His lips twitched. "Okay. Animal enough for you?"

"It was most satisfactory, but perhaps next time we should do as the animals do."

He broke into a wide smile. "I'm with ya. Doggie style."

"Chimp style," she corrected and immediately clamped her mouth shut.

He studied her for a moment, which made her squirm. She really didn't want to share her chimp findings on him just yet. She'd yet to finish the experiment, and she still needed to analyze the data and search for patterns. Besides, she suspected he might not like the comparison. He was touchy about the strangest things. They were, after all, primates. To distract him, she dropped to the floor and went on all fours, offering herself in a nice open way like a female chimp would.

"Fuck," he muttered. "If only I could. You're killing me, Kate. Tonight."

She smiled to herself, stood, and headed to the foyer in search of the purple panties that matched her bra.

"Ah, Kate," Ian called. "I don't have my boxer briefs yet, do I?"

She huffed. "You'll get them tonight." She snagged her panties, but before she could get them on, Ian was there.

He snatched them away and grinned. "You'll get them back when I get mine."

"You won't even know if I'm commando or not, you'll be at work."

"Oh, I'll know." He kissed her. "I better get ready." He headed to the bedroom, her panties twirling around his finger. *Argh.*

She had a drawer full of panties in the bedroom, but he was in there, so she'd wait. For now she'd let him think he got his way. The male ego required boosting sometimes, she'd observed.

She trailed back to the sofa and found her clothes. She pulled her shorts on first. Actually, this didn't feel so bad without the panties. The shorts were a soft cotton. She sat to reach for her bra on the floor and ooh! This commando thing felt kinda nice. "Mmm," she said.

Ian chuckled, returning to the living room, where he was zipping up his black pants over his new black metaphorical reminder boxers. His shirt was draped across his forearm, and he held his socks and shoes in one hand. "I wanted to watch you dress. You like being commando?"

She tipped her head up to look at him. "Mmm-hmmm."

"Why did you say chimp style?" he asked, dropping the shoes and socks and pulling on a black button-down shirt. "I've never heard it called that."

She stood abruptly. Her breasts bounced from the sudden movement, which had the unintended effect of drawing his attention to her chest. *Note: breasts are a good male distraction.* He seemed to have forgotten his chimp question. That gave her time to steer the conversation to an important topic.

"I have your question for today." She'd been tackling one important topic per day, which was her condensed version of the twelve-part experiment. They were on the ninth part. She was cautiously optimistic about the results. Some things were still troubling and/or puzzling. The territoriality issue being at the top of the list. Also what was the deal with the mixed-nut jar? Why did he get mad that she ate all the cashews? Why did they have to be eaten in random handfuls? Wasn't the point of a mixed-nut jar to choose what you felt like eating?

He closed the space between them, his gaze never leaving her breasts. "Yeah, what?"

"What's the most important thing to you in a relationship?"

"Nudity." Eyes still glued to her breasts.

She crossed her arms. "You said you'd take our science experiment seriously."

He reached out with both hands and pinched her nipples, sending a rush of electric pleasure through her. She dropped her arms and watched as his thumb and forefinger on both of his large hands rolled her nipples and then tugged. Her knees went weak as her breath left her in a whoosh. "Please," she whispered.

He dropped his hands and held her by the shoulders a foot away. "You're insatiable."

"It's your fault," she countered.

He gave her his lopsided smile and retrieved his shoes and socks. "Put your clothes on if you want a better answer from me. I can't think when you're naked."

She quickly put on her bra and shirt because she really did need to get part nine figured out. "Okay, I'm dressed. Now tell me the most important thing to you in a relationship."

He bent down and tied his shoes. "Honesty."

She beamed and padded over to him in her bare feet. "I'm always honest."

He looked up at her and gave her a warm smile. "Then you must be the most important thing in a relationship."

She blinked, momentarily stunned. And then her heart filled to bursting. Like she could just float away on a cloud of love. Wow.

He stood, gave her a quick kiss, grabbed his laptop bag from the foyer table, and opened the door. "See ya tonight, and you'd better be commando," he threw over his shoulder and left.

Swoon!

She rushed back to her laptop. *Male's words of praise weigh heavily with female. Reciprocity is in order.*

Four hours later, Kate showed up at Ian's work with a pretty silver gift bag decorated with hearts containing his lunch. She'd picked up his favorite ranch chicken sandwich from his favorite neighborhood place and put it in the gift bag so it would be a surprise. On the short train ride over to the MIT campus, she tried to think of the best words of praise for whatever it was Ian did at work. She came up with *fantastic, impressive,* and *very nice.* Those would work well for any level of technological sophistication she found at the lab. It helped to have words at the ready in new situations; otherwise she got lost in thought and people sometimes took offense, thinking she wasn't paying attention. The problem was she paid too much attention, which made her think deeply.

She reminded herself to buy him more boxer briefs later

since he was so attached to them. She'd pulled on another pair of panties from her drawer (Ian had kindly emptied two drawers for her for their captivity experiment). She figured Ian wouldn't notice if she wasn't commando at his work. It wasn't like he'd be groping her there or peeking in her shorts to check.

When she got to the lab, a standalone two-story brick building at the edge of the MIT campus, she buzzed to be let in. She peered through the glass in the top half of the door and saw a tall woman walking by. Kate buzzed again, and the woman turned and headed straight toward her. Short sleek black hair, sharp brown eyes, high cheekbones, slender with big breasts. Kate swallowed hard, shocked and hurt and angry all at once. She had no idea that *she* worked here. But there was no time for a freak-out because the beautiful woman was almost at the door.

Kate braced herself for impact.

The woman pulled open the door, her brown eyes direct. "Kate, I wondered when you'd show up."

Kate stood face-to-face with Ian's girlfriend of three years. Ex-girlfriend. The woman who'd given him an ultimatum and been dumped over it. The same woman who wouldn't let Ian spend time with Kate as a friend because she knew that Ian and Kate had a history.

Kate drew herself up to her full five foot two since the other woman towered over her. "Hello, Morgan. I'm unsure if Ian has informed you of this, but we are now engaged to be married." Dammit. She always got too formal when she was upset.

Morgan stared at her for a long moment. "I have been informed." Her lips curled into a smile that didn't reach her eyes. "You look shocked to see me. Ha! I can't wait to hear Ian talk his way out of this one."

She turned and stalked off to where Kate assumed Ian worked. Kate followed, her heart racing, her mind chaotic with all the implications. How long had Morgan been working with Ian? Was this why he took the job? Was she his boss or vice versa? And also what the hell!

What the ever-loving hell! Was this honesty? The most important thing in a relationship? Morgan was back in his life? How long had this been going on?

"Look who I found," Morgan caroled, peeking into a glass office. She yanked Kate front and center. "Your *friend* Kate."

Ian startled from where he sat at his desk. His gaze darted from Morgan to Kate and back to Morgan.

Kate was so furious, so beside herself, she didn't even know where to begin.

"Go back to work, Morgan," Ian said.

Morgan just stood there, smirking. "She sure looked surprised to see me. Guess you didn't tell her about you being my boss. How you especially sought me out as a new hire. What all that means."

Kate's jaw dropped. The gift bag hit the floor, falling from her limp hand.

"Stop it," Ian snapped at Morgan. "Get out of my office."

Ian turned to her. "Kate—"

"Bonobo!" Kate hollered, whirled and stomped away. A bonobo was a monkey that used sex to get what it wanted. She used to think he was a nice alpha chimp, but no-o-o-o, everything was clear now.

Ian was a bonobo with a capital B.

# 11

"Kate, wait!" Ian took off after Kate. He knew this looked bad, but he could explain. Morgan was stirring up shit. She'd always been jealous of Kate. Always accused him of lying when he said they were just friends. "Slow down!" he called because Kate was practically running.

She peeked over her shoulder and yelled, "No!" Then she turned, slammed into Shawn Vogel, who had at least two hundred pounds on her, and bounced. Her arms windmilled, but Shawn grabbed her and held her upright.

Shawn, with his short dark brown hair and neatly trimmed beard, was a favorite among the women in the AI lab. A rare specimen—the body of a linebacker, the sharp mind of an engineer. He smiled down at her. "Hey, cutie, where's the fire?"

Kate stared, eyes wide. "Who are you?"

"Shawn Vogel. I work engineering on the driverless cars."

"Kate," she breathed.

"I got her," Ian said, tugging Kate out of Shawn's beefy hands.

Kate yanked away from Ian. "Leave me alone."

"Got yourself a little spitfire," Shawn said. "You know what to do with all that fire?"

"Mind your business," Ian snapped.

Shawn winked at Kate. "Because I do."

Kate tittered and smoothed her hair. "Thank you, Shawn Vogel. If you'll excuse me, I really must be going."

She turned to go, and Ian grabbed her hand before she could make her escape. "I want to talk to you in private," he said.

Kate scowled and muttered, "Stupid bonobo."

Shawn grinned. "Later."

Ian lifted his chin at Shawn and turned back to Kate. She was glaring at him. At least she wasn't gazing after Shawn. "Let's go outside to talk."

She walked with him, muttering the whole time about reciprocity and the complete breakdown of the primate communication system, which made no sense, but he figured he should just let her get it out.

When they got outside, he took both of her hands for their talk so she couldn't get away. "Morgan was just trying to make you jealous because she's always been jealous of you."

"Why is she here?"

"She's got a contract to work on the space project."

"So you're her boss?"

"In a way. She has to keep me and Dr. Wilson up to date on her progress, but she's a contractor, so her boss is still her boss from the company where she works."

She yanked her hands free. "Uh-huh. And where is this all-important *honesty* in our relationship, huh?"

"I didn't lie about anything."

"You never told me your beautiful ex-girlfriend was working with you!" she shouted at the top of her lungs. "Stupid bonobo! Stupid! Stupid! Stupid!" She paced back and forth and then jabbed a finger at him. "This is going in my report."

He was somehow missing something really important here, but he wasn't sure what. "Why do you keep calling me a bonobo? What is that?"

She glared at him and spoke through her teeth. "A bonobo is a monkey that uses sex as currency to get what it wants. I used to think you were like a nice alpha chimp, but you are clearly the bonobo brand of monkey."

He scratched his head. "Okay, monkeys?"

"Yes!"

He let that one slide. "I don't use sex as currency."

"You use sex to get what you want and to avoid communication, which is the cornerstone of a solid relationship!"

He looked around, hoping her voice wasn't carrying back to anyone in the lab. He lowered his voice, hoping she'd lower hers too. "I don't need to use sex to get what I want from you. I get what I want just from being with you."

She crossed her arms. "How long has she been here?" At least her volume was back to normal.

"Just started today."

"Then why did she make it sound like she'd been here a while? She said and I quote, 'Kate, I wondered when you'd show up,' like she'd already been here a long time."

He pulled her into his arms, and she didn't wrap her arms around him, but she didn't pull away either. "I told you she was messing with you. She always accused me of having more-than-friends kind of feelings for you. And you know she had good reason to be jealous because I did. You've always had my heart no matter how far apart we were or how many people were between us."

She rested her head on his chest. He stayed quiet, knowing she liked to listen to his heart beat and that it calmed her. She looked up at him, her blue eyes direct through her glasses. "Why didn't you tell me she was going to be working here?"

"I was going to tell you once she started."

"Why wait?"

"I don't know. I guess I figured there was nothing to talk about until it happened."

"For future reference I would like to know stuff the moment it happens."

"Okay, so noted. See, this is good communication. No sex involved."

She grimaced. "So she just started today and you told her we were engaged."

"Yes."

"Did she ask if you were involved with someone, or you offered this information?"

He thought quick. Morgan had cornered him in the break room, where he was getting coffee and said she'd missed him. He'd immediately told her he was engaged. How much should he tell Kate? He didn't want her to worry unnecessarily. He took one look at Kate's direct gaze and decided to be like Kate—honest to the very last detail. He told her exactly what happened word for word.

Kate swallowed and looked over his shoulder. "She's very pretty. And smart."

He cupped her jaw and turned her back to him. "So are you."

"Ian, you're biased because I sleep with you. I'm not that pretty. Morgan looks like a model—"

He slid a hand into her hair and gazed into her eyes. "You're the most beautiful sexy woman I've ever met. Honest."

Her bottom lip stuck out in a pout. "But I'm not tall and thin."

"You're petite and curvy. Believe me, that works for a guy."

"My hair's always messy. Hers was in a sleek stylish cut."

He stroked her hair, admiring the shades of gold and the shine. It was in a messy half bun, as usual, only he got to see it loose and flowing in bed. He loved that. "Guys like long hair. Trust me on that too. I love pulling out your hair band and running my fingers through it."

"I'm a nerd."

He met her eyes and grinned. "So am I."

She snort-laughed.

He pulled her close and kissed her. "I love you. And nothing you can say will convince me otherwise."

Her eyes got shiny. "I love you too."

"C'mon, you want to see what we're working on?" He

entwined his fingers with hers and tugged her back to the door.

"How long will Morgan be working here?"

"Contract is for a year."

"Great."

Ian walked ahead of her, slid his ID card over the sensor, and opened the door. "What made you stop by today?"

"Reciprocity," she replied.

He joined her in the hallway. "Because I visited your lab?"

"No, because you said something sweet about me being important in a relationship, so I wanted to do something nice. I brought you lunch."

He tensed. "Did you, uh, cook?"

She smacked his arm. "You can relax. You're not going to get food poisoning. I brought you takeout. Your favorite ranch chicken sandwich."

"Aww, thanks." He walked down the hallway. "You know who would make a good couple?"

"Who?"

"Morgan and Nate."

"Nate's much too nice for her."

"Not really."

"Ian! He's one of the nicest guys I know. Morgan's an instigator and *not* the good kind!"

"Well, this instigator is going to be spending a lot of time with your fiancé," Morgan said, appearing behind them.

Kate turned. "You're a liar! Hold me back, Ian." She pulled her elbows back for him, and he obligingly held Kate back. Not that she'd have a chance against the much larger Morgan. "I'm gonna go gorilla on her ass!"

"Stupid bitch," Morgan muttered and brushed past them, heading toward the stairs.

"Morgan," Ian snapped, "apologize to Kate or you'll be meeting with Dr. Wilson about your future here."

Morgan stopped halfway down the stairs and turned. "Sorry," she muttered.

"Your apology is accepted in the manner in which it was

given," Kate said. "Halfheartedly and with no sincerity whatsoever."

Kate turned in the opposite direction of Morgan, and Ian followed. God, he loved this woman.

Kate toured the lab, impressed with the work they were doing there. She wasn't happy about Morgan's employment, but the woman was clearly not on Ian's good side with her name-calling, so there was that. Of course, Kate had called her an instigator, but that was behind her back, so really shouldn't count.

She toured the second floor, where a lot of PhD students worked under Ian's supervision on a variety of social robots. There were robots of varying appearances, some cuddly, some like funny fuzzy aliens, some more people-like (but without hair) for such varied applications as teaching foreign languages, companionship for terminally ill children, and the one that really got to her was the trust robot. It was used as an intermediary so children who might not be comfortable confiding in a therapist could confide in the robot programmed with questions with a therapist nearby. Kate could've used a trust robot like that to confide in as a kid. Not that she had a lot of dark secrets. She'd just wanted a friend to talk to during the long lonely afternoons before her parents got home. The first floor had offices and computer stations as well as an open floor area used to test robotic pets made of projected lights, digital painting made by dancing feet, and some mobile talking robots.

Ian stopped at the stairs leading to the lower level. "This is where Morgan works. Are you sure you want to see her?"

"Of course. If she's going to be working here, I'm sure I'll see her regularly." Kate was not about to let Morgan's presence deter her from touring the entire facility. Besides, she wanted to show Morgan that Kate and Ian were a united chimp front. Never mind that the two chimps hadn't yet successfully completed the experiment and had issues.

"You don't have to," Ian said.

"Please, Ian, stop coddling me. I can handle it."

"All right."

She followed him down to a large open space. Half the space was for a car, where Shawn, the huge guy she'd run into earlier, worked with a couple of other guys. The other half had a large squat pile of metal with multiple extended arms that she assumed was for the space program because the lying bitch was working over there with three other people.

She headed for Morgan first to show Ian that it was no problem whatsoever for the mature woman he was going to marry.

"Hi, guys," Ian said. "This is my fiancée, Kate. I'm just showing her around."

The two men and one woman that worked with Morgan said hi. Morgan gave her a small smile that was downright chilling.

"We meet again," Morgan said. And she might as well have added *bwa-ha-ha* for the evil vibe she was giving off.

Ian explained how this was the most sophisticated robot used to date in the space program, designed to take a human's place on space walks. He pointed out the various features as Kate tried to listen and not notice Morgan's scrutiny of Kate's clothes. Kate wore a simple purple cotton T-shirt and black cotton shorts. She hadn't thought twice about her outfit and hadn't noticed Morgan's either, but now she was noticing. Morgan wore a navy blazer over a white silk shirt with a pale pink rose, and skinny navy blue pants that tapered at the ankles. She wore gold metallic heels. No wonder the woman towered over Kate in her sneakers.

Morgan moved to a laptop in the corner of the room, and Kate let out a breath of relief.

"C'mon, Kate," Ian said, tugging her over to the car.

"There she is!" Shawn exclaimed. "Ready to check her out? Hop in."

Kate flushed. Shawn opened the passenger-side door for her and gestured for her to get in. She slipped inside, and he got in the driver's side. Ian peered in through the window on her side.

"So this is Ike," Shawn said, pointing to a small robot face on the dashboard with a cell phone connected to the base. "He's plugged into both the phone and the car. He can do navigation, check the vehicle's systems, and check your messages." He grinned. "I'm working on some conversational abilities too. A relaxed driver is a good driver."

"I thought this was a driverless car," Kate said.

"This one can go either way. You can program it to do the drive, or you can use it as a driver assistant."

"Cool!" she exclaimed.

"How's the traffic avoidance working?" Ian asked.

"Yeah, I wanted to have you take a look at that." Shawn got out of the car. Kate looked around the car for a bit, it mostly looked like a regular car, and then she got out too. Ian was bent over a computer, looking at something with Shawn.

Kate wandered over to the other side of the room, thinking about the importance of Ian's work—useful applications that could make people's lives better. Was that more important than understanding the universe? Her work didn't have immediate life-changing effects. What was an objective way of determining career precedence? Given two equally important jobs in two very different fields, did it really just come down to money?

"So what's your secret?" a woman's voice asked.

Kate jumped and whirled to find Morgan standing behind her. "Secret?"

Morgan slid a look over to Ian, whose back was to them, and back to her. "How'd you get him to commit? You've been together how long? A year and a half? Since me and Ian broke up, I bet."

"Five months," Kate corrected automatically. She couldn't tolerate inaccuracies in numbers.

Morgan raised a brow. "I'm surprised he waited at all. So five months and you're engaged. I was with him *three years,* and the moment I mentioned marriage, he cut me loose. So what's your secret?" Her gaze dropped to Kate's flat stomach. Like a pregnancy was the only reason Ian would marry her!

Kate raised her chin. "Well, I didn't give him an ultimatum."

Morgan's lip curled. "So he just proposed all on his own?"

"I asked him, and he said yes."

Morgan barked out a laugh. "You asked him?" She lowered her voice. "Idiot. He didn't want to say no. I bet he's hemming and hawing, trying to get out of it. Did he tell you he has cold feet?"

Kate pressed her lips together. Ian was still bent over a computer screen. She would not bolt. She had to stand her ground. "This is none of your concern."

"Oh my God, he did! Well, guess what? That's step one. Step two is out the door." She walked her fingers in the air.

"You're wrong," Kate said firmly. Though she felt a small niggle of worry.

"Unless he doesn't have the balls. Then he'll just leave you at the altar."

Kate's stomach dropped. The idea of planning her dream fairy-tale wedding only to be left standing in her beautiful poufy dress and tiara was horrifying.

"I must be going now," Kate replied stiffly and headed toward Ian.

"Good luck," Morgan called. "I sure don't envy you."

She arrived at Ian's side, nearly vibrating with tension. She knew Morgan was jealous, knew she was a liar, yet she was shaken up. Ian did have cold feet. Their experiment was not at all positively conclusive. Oh God. What if he did leave her at the altar? How could she be sure of him?

"Hey," Ian said, turning to her. "Almost done here."

"No need to hurry," she said. She could feel her formal tone taking over, but she was too worked up to fight it. "I'll be heading out now. Thank you for the informative tour of the facility. Enjoy your ranch chicken sandwich in its decorative gift bag."

Ian's head swiveled back to her. "What's wrong?"

"Nothing is wrong. I've intruded long enough, and I have

work of my own to attend to." She kissed his cheek so he'd be sure to know she really could handle seeing his ex-girlfriend and was a mature well-balanced partner. "I'll see you this evening."

She turned to go, and he snagged her around the waist, hauling her back. "Hold up. Five minutes, and I'll have lunch with you."

She tried to move away, and he snagged the elastic waist-band at the back of her shorts. "I'm not hungry," she said in as dignified a voice as she could muster, given the gap from his hand to her exposed back was giving everyone a peep at her purple panties. She eased a step closer to him, hoping to close the gap. "But thank you for the kind invitation."

She tried to twist sideways out of his grip, and Ian's arm banded around her waist, hauling her in front of him. She pushed at his arm, and he tightened his hold. Her cheeks burned as Shawn smiled at the exchange. She stared at the screen that had Ian's attention, pretending this was all perfectly normal. But she saw nothing. Lines of code that blurred in front of her watery eyes. Ian's voice rumbled at her back for a few minutes while she told herself Morgan was just messing with her and she couldn't let her get in her head. But the hard truth was that Ian did have cold feet. And that was enough to give credibility to Ian walking out on her at any moment, even the last possible moment, and, if she was honest with herself, that was the whole reason she'd come up with an experiment in the first place.

And they were doing terribly! Every time a disagreement came up, Ian used her short circuit to shut her up. They had sex entirely too much of the time when they should've been establishing good communication systems and negotiating domestic life. They hadn't talked about anything important at all! They lived on take-out food, the laundry was piling up, and while Kate wasn't Miss Neat by any measure, his apart-ment was a disaster area! There were always whiskers in the sink, toothpaste gobs on the counter, he drank very unhygien-ically straight from the milk carton, and half his dirty socks were on the floor *next* to the hamper because, for some strange reason, he liked to toss them in from a distance like a basketball player. And if he missed, there they stayed. Total dirty gross disaster area, and she refused to clean up after him just because she was the female.

Ian's grip on her loosened and his voice rumbled in her ear, sending hot tingling vibrations through her despite her agitation. "All right," he said all sexy-like. "Let's go have lunch."

That was the problem with Ian. Sexing everything up all the time when they had important issues to work through. She pulled him away from the group and said as quietly as possible, "Sex doesn't solve everything!"

Ian cocked his head. "I have a feeling you want to talk." He pulled her quickly toward the stairs.

She walked stiffly. "Yes, we have a lot to talk about."

"Can it wait until tonight?"

"Yes, of course," she replied cordially because she was a mature well-balanced partner. "Enjoy your ranch chicken sandwich in its decorative gift bag. I'll see you tonight in the living room, where we will have our conversation."

She pulled her hand free, rushed up the stairs, and saw her escape. Through the hallway, out the front door. She didn't want Ian to see how much Morgan got to her. She was dimly aware that Morgan probably saw her fleeing, but her need for escape trumped everything. By tonight she'd be calmed down enough for a rational conversation. Maybe she'd make a list of topics they needed to address. Communication topped the list.

She reached the door, grabbed the handle, and flew backwards into hard male chest.

"Not so fast, Dr. Lewis," Ian growled, his arms wrapping around her chest, pinning her arms to her sides.

Ian's formal tone told her two things—he was mad, and he was onto her.

She still tried to make a break for it, wriggling against his hold before she finally gave up. He was bigger and stronger, so she must use her wits. Her own tone would tell him everything he needed to know. "Dr. Furnukle, this is neither the time nor the place. Please release your hold and we will have our important conversation this evening."

"Talk."

"Not here," she said through her teeth.

"I'm going to let you go to open the door, but if you bolt on me, I will catch you, toss you over my shoulder, and we'll have this conversation outside on the MIT campus, where everyone can see my monkey girlfriend hanging upside down to talk. You'll be the monkey, Kate. Not me."

"Ian!"

"And my hand will be on your ass the entire time."

"Ian!" Dammit. He was turning her on. "Stop being a bonobo."

"Don't push me, Kate. I swear I'll do it."

"Okay, okay."

He let go of her and pulled open the door. She bolted.

**12**

———

Kate ran like a crazed squirrel, veering left and right, hoping to outmaneuver him even if she couldn't outrun him. She was in a crazy mental place between exhilaration at the chase and pure mortification over her inability to deal with his ex. His legs were much longer, giving him an unfair advantage. She ran diagonally across campus; luckily she knew the place from her graduate studies. She was starting to get winded, peeked over her shoulder, saw he was nearly on her, and tripped on a tree root. She flailed; then she was falling, about to kiss the ground when he grabbed her and hauled her upright. His arms wrapped around her, her back pressed against his chest. She could tell he was winded too from the way his chest heaved against her.

"Seriously," he huffed. "This is how you want to play this?"

She decided the unexpected was her best strategy to avoid the humiliation of an upside-down hand-on-her-ass talk. "Yes. I greatly enjoy your hand on my ass, so I would like you to haul me over your shoulder, spread your hand as wide as possible on my ass, maybe a light spanking while you're at it, and talk to me about our issues."

His chest shook with laughter. "Geez, Kate, you slay me." He leaned down and kissed her temple. "Why're you so upset?" he asked gently. "Did Morgan say something to you?"

She swallowed. "Nothing I didn't know already."

He turned her in his arms. "Which is?"

"That cold feet lead to being left."

"Exactly how does that work?"

She spoke to his chest. "You know."

"I don't know. I never said I was leaving you. Maybe that's what Morgan wants, but it's not what I want."

"We're not doing so well." She pointed out the obvious. Sometimes the male missed those obvious cues.

"How so?"

"We're only on day nine and our communication sucks, we have entirely too much sex, which you use to shut me up, don't deny it!" She warmed to her topic. "Neither one of us has stepped up in domestic life. No one has cooked, the laundry is piling up, and your apartment is a disaster area!"

He put his hands on his hips. "You're the one who made the apartment a disaster area! Shaving cream all over the walls!"

"Whiskers in the sink!"

"Lipstick all over the mirror!"

"Toothpaste gobs on the counter!"

He jabbed a finger at her. "Equations everywhere! Even on food." He narrowed his eyes. "I found sigma carved into the butter."

"That was a derivative function!" She scowled. "You drink from the carton."

"At least I buy groceries. You just wander around the city, forget what you're supposed to get, and come home."

"It's called thinking, you ape!"

"What is with all the monkey stuff?"

"Nothing."

He slowly shook his head and then grabbed her.

"Ah!" she screamed as he tossed her over his shoulder, his hand landing on her ass with a smack. "Ian!" The blood rushed to her head. People were starting to stare.

She smacked his ass a bunch of times. He ignored her.

"You're the monkey now," he said. "Tell me why you're obsessed with monkeys, my little bonobo."

"I just like animals."

His fingers spread wide on her ass. "Wrong answer."

Dammit. This getting-turned-on-in-public thing was not how she pictured their lunch together today. "Your ranch chicken sandwich should probably be refrigerated."

"Ba-diddy-dum," he sang in time to the rhythm he played on her bottom with his palm.

"Ian," she moaned.

"Oh, what's that? My little bonobo turned on? Great. Let's talk about our issues."

She clamped her mouth shut.

He played some mysterious rhythm on her ass while he walked, carrying her behind a building to a parking lot. He didn't set her down. Instead he spoke casually, his hand still firmly on her ass, holding her like a sack of rice. Honestly, if she knew this was what being engaged would be like, she wasn't so sure she would've signed up for it. Ian just wouldn't fall in line the way he was supposed to. He was supposed to be playing the part of devoted, besotted fiancé. Not an angry chimp with pseudo-bonobo tones. This would all be going in her report.

"Kate!"

"Huh?"

"Did you hear a word I said?"

"Yes."

"Repeat it back to me."

"You would like to sincerely apologize for the upside-down hand-on-my-ass talk, and furthermore you will do your best not to be a slob, will learn to cook for both of us, will go to a couples therapist to establish better communications systems, and will fire Morgan so I never have to see her again." All the couples in the marriage literature had couples therapists with very positive outcomes.

"Ba-dum-bum," he said, playing a comic drumroll on her ass. "Good one, Kate. What did I really say?"

"You appreciate all my quirks and understand that equations happen anywhere and everywhere and that's part of my process."

He set her back on her feet and gazed at her for a long moment. She was quiet, waiting for the blood to settle back in her body. Unfortunately, she was still turned on. But that couldn't be helped. Ian had an animal appeal that her body responded to whether or not her brain was on board.

"Kate, you're not easy to live with," he finally said.

She scowled. "Neither are you."

"But I do appreciate your quirks." He cupped her jaw, his fingers warm on her cheek. "I fell in love with you because you're unique. You fascinate me, excite me, surprise me. I always want to know what you're thinking. I always want to talk to you and touch you and, yes, fuck you. A lot."

Her throat got tight, her eyes hot. "Ian," she said softly, "we still need to—"

"We'll do whatever we need to do. I'm calling it, Kate. Experiment's over. I'm all in."

"But—"

His other hand cupped her jaw, framing her face with his hands. "Trial run is over. Love wins." He gazed deep into her eyes. "We both win."

She was speechless. She couldn't believe he took that leap of faith without any data to back him up. She hadn't even presented her findings. They still had three topics to get through.

His lips met hers, warm and tender, and her brain shut down. She melted against him, relief flooding her. His arms wrapped around her waist, and his lips pressed against her hair as he enfolded her in a long embrace. She wrapped her arms around his waist and squeezed tight.

A few moments later, he pulled back and met her eyes. "We good now?"

She nodded, too choked up to manage anything else.

He took her hand and started walking back toward his office.

She finally found her voice. "I'm sorry I called you a bonobo."

"Ditto."

"Can I still share my experimental findings with you?"

"I'd love to hear them."

"They're set in an animal framework, but we are primates, you know."

He stopped short, and she saw the moment understanding dawned. "Two chimps in love that we don't know. That's what you meant! You've been observing us like two chimps."

She beamed, so glad he really got her.

"You know I'm the alpha chimp," he said, continuing their walk.

"That's not always a good thing," she muttered.

"Oo-oo-oo-ah-ah!" Ian's chimp impersonation was quite good. Kate flushed as heads turned. Then he grabbed her around the waist and lifted her, carrying her against his front. She wrapped her arms and legs around him like a chimp. "There's my little monkey," he crooned in her ear.

"There's my giant monkey," she returned.

"Damn right."

She buried her face in his neck, breathing him in. Love won. For the first time since she'd arrived in Boston, her entire body relaxed. Just in time too. There were a number of wedding planning items coming up very soon. She'd been hoping things between them would go well enough to actually follow through. Tomorrow she had a girls' day out in Clover Park (her sister's idea) for wedding gown shopping with her sister, mom, and mother-in-law. Ian only knew it was a girls' day out, not the purpose of the outing, and he still didn't know about the party.

She lifted her head. "Amber has arranged for our engagement party the Saturday before I go back to Chicago."

He stopped short. "In two weeks?"

"Yes."

"Since when has this been planned?"

"Since March?"

"Is that a question?"

"No?"

He sighed and murmured, "Always a surprise."

"I didn't want to mention it and add bias or undue pressure to our captivity experiment. Also, the purpose of girls' day out is to find a wedding gown."

"Ah," he said, and then much louder, "captivity!" His shoulders shook, and she realized he was laughing. "Monkeys! Is that what you've been working on your laptop all this time? Data and monkey observations?"

"Of course not. I'm a serious physicist. I have important work to do."

"I want to see what you've got on us tonight."

"I'll prepare a report."

"You do that, Kate. I'd really like to read it."

She hugged him tight with her arms and legs, knowing she'd pleased him.

Ian was not pleased. He'd returned home after work to find a ten-page report waiting for him with detailed observations on him and suggested solutions to *his* issues. Territoriality? Alpha displays? *Perceived* high-value items? Maybe he needed shaving cream and underwear! Mixed-nut fetish? Animal drive? Well, that wasn't too bad. Wait, what was this? Hostile tone and stance? This was how Kate saw him?

"Hostile?" he barked. "I'm not hostile!"

She pushed her glasses up. "These are merely observations of real-life events."

He scanned the report, searching for anything complimentary at all. Nothing on *him*. But everything on the female was most complimentary. Female adapted to environment. Female used resources well. Completely biased!

He turned to her sitting next to him on the sofa, looking all superior. "This report is flawed. In fact, your whole experiment is flawed."

"What? That's impossible! I was very careful to keep an objective distance from two chimps in love that I never met."

"Then why do I look like a snarling ape and you look like a well-adjusted completely harmonious chimp?"

She pushed her hair behind her ears. "Like I said, those are just observations of real-life events."

"I'm not hostile!"

"Perhaps some video feedback would be useful."

He ground his teeth. "I'm not territorial either. In fact, I don't think you could find a much more laid-back guy than me."

She snorted.

"You used all my shaving cream," he said.

"Which I replaced."

"You threw out my boxer briefs."

"Which I replaced with an alternative."

"You ate all the cashews."

She sighed and rolled her eyes. "This is exactly what I'm talking about. I believe it's your perceived lack of resources causing this territoriality problem. If you could just make a list of what you consider high value, I could stockpile those items and—"

"Any guy would be irritated living with you!"

She blinked and her lips pressed into a flat line. "Perhaps you're right. I've never lived with a man before. Perhaps I'm ill-suited to such an arrangement." She folded her hands in her lap and stared at them.

Now he felt like an ass. He put an arm around her shoulders and pulled her close. "You're not ill-suited or whatever. We'll work it out."

She looked up at him. "Perhaps a couples therapist could help us establish effective communication systems. It's in all the literature."

"We don't need that. We communicate just fine."

She straightened. "Maybe it's good that we'll have a little time apart tomorrow." She took off her glasses and cleaned them industriously with the end of her T-shirt. "It will give us both some perspective and a chance to calm down enough for a rational conversation."

He didn't know what to say to that. She was probably right, but he had a feeling if he agreed that some time apart would be good, she might take it the wrong way. So he said nothing.

Kate slid her glasses back on. "Maybe I'll spend the night in Clover Park too."

She was taking his car to drive down tomorrow. He could either go with her and wait around while she did all her girl stuff, or he could let her go and maybe her sister would make her see reason in her biased view of their captivity experiment. He quickly decided the best thing to do was agree with whatever she said.

"Sure, if that's what you want," he said. "I'll catch up on some paperwork. Have fun."

She stood abruptly. "I need to call my sister."

He let her go. She probably wanted to firm up the details for the weekend. Kate liked a planned agenda.

He slouched down on the sofa, put his feet up on the coffee table, and pulled out his cell phone to play some games. *Captivity experiment*. He shook his head.

Kate went into the bedroom and shut the door. A few moments later, he caught snippets of Kate's side of the conversation. "Complete break…all in…refuses couples therapy…won't fall in line."

He sat up straight, his feet hitting the floor. Fall in line! If anyone was going to fall in line in this relationship, it was Kate. She had to adapt to him a whole helluva lot better before she had anything to say about him adapting to her. He put up with a lot!

She got quiet for a while, so she must've been listening. He hoped Amber was setting her straight. Then he heard her say, "That would be a long list."

He crossed to the door and pounded on it. He was surprised when it swung open. He thought he'd have to convince her to open it.

"Oh, fine," Kate said into the phone, "but I already told you everything." She sighed. "Here." She handed him the phone. Great. Now his sister-in-law would ream him out.

He snatched the phone and barked, "My fiancée should be the one talking to me!"

"Hey now," Barry said. "Let's take it down a notch."

Kate brushed by him and returned to the living room. She pulled out her laptop and started typing, probably observing more of his hostility.

"Why are you butting in?" Ian asked.

"Amber loves you guys. She wants you both to be happy. Kate helped her over a rough patch in our relationship. That meant a lot to her."

"So Amber put you up to it?"

"She thought a man-to-man talk would help."

"You are so whipped."

"Happily so."

Ian scrubbed a hand over his face. He did *not* want to be turning this into a whole family thing.

"She feels you're hostile," Barry said.

"I'm not—"

"You're loud. Women take that to heart."

He studied Kate, who was looking serious, typing like crazy. He'd never thought of her as all that sensitive, but maybe under her serious scientific exterior, she was. And he'd been beating his chest like a gorilla.

Barry went on. "Come down on Saturday. That's an order, not a request."

"Or what?"

"Or Amber will kick your ass."

Ian laughed, though his petite sister-in-law was tough when she needed to be. "In that case, I'd better brush up on my kung fu."

Barry chuckled.

"We're fine," Ian said, "but thanks."

"Listen," Barry said, his voice lowering, "you helped me out with Amber, remember? You told me to ditch the Hawaiian shirts. You encouraged me to get back to my acting roots to get a much-needed confidence boost. It helped Amber see me in a new light. Now I want to return the favor. I'm on your side."

He blew out a breath. "She wants to have a girls' weekend, so that's what she's going to get."

"She wants you."

"She said—forget it. I don't want to talk to you about this. I know you mean well, but no. I gotta go." He went to hang up, but he still heard his brother's last buttinski move.

"She's worth it!" Barry called.

Ian rolled his eyes and hung up. Seriously. Just because Barry was happily married, happily whipped, happily everything didn't mean Ian wanted him as a go-between. He and Kate would be fine. She said she wanted a weekend away for perspective, so he'd give her what she wanted.

He turned and gazed at Kate—his unique, aggravating, sexy-as-all-hell fiancée. Then he crossed to her, returned her cell phone, and sat next to her on the sofa.

She quickly shut the laptop and set it on the coffee table. He was sure she'd been working on more hostile chimp observations on him.

He took her hand. "I'm sorry for my hostile tone."

"You're forgiven."

"Are you writing more stuff about me?"

"Barry suggested I create a bug report on our relationship. You know, a list of the flaws so we can work through them in a systematic way. I told him it would be a long list."

He stifled a groan. Classic software engineer solution to the problem. He could only imagine what was on her long list.

Kate went on. "You should work on your report as well to address any bugs from your perspective. We can tackle them when I return from my weekend away."

"Okay." He might be able to think of a few. Bug report number one: my fiancée enjoys observing me like a chimp.

"We only have thirty days to get it right," she said in a flat tone. She retrieved her laptop. "Actually, seventeen days left to get it right." This was true. She flew back to Chicago at the end of the month. "Or not," she added.

He felt a little queasy, though he couldn't quite put his finger on why. Was it the running-out-of-time thing? Her flat tone, like she'd already given up? The fact that she had a long list of relationship flaws to catalogue, by which she probably meant Ian flaws?

But wait, the whole reason she was going to Clover Park was to shop for a wedding gown. That had to be good. She must ultimately believe that they'd work things out. Right?

## 13

———

Kate drove to Clover Park with an unwanted passenger—
Doom. The impending sense of doom clinging to her was so
strong, crushing her tender heart, it felt like a physical presence in the car.

Ian should *not* have let her go so easily. Knowing they
only had seventeen days left (as she'd reminded him) before
another long separation, possibly even a year separation if
she got the Geneva fellowship, he should have *wanted* to join
her this weekend. Instead, paperwork had taken priority. And
not just any paperwork. Morgan's paperwork for a grant
application. He'd informed her this morning he'd be meeting
with Morgan over coffee to go over it.

*Stop it*, she told herself. *It's just work.*

*He chose working with Morgan over you*, Doom said from the
passenger seat.

*No, it was all last minute. Ian didn't plan any of that.* He was
assistant director of the lab. He'd likely meet up with anyone
who needed it on a Saturday morning coffee date.

She ground her teeth. *Not a date.*

*He had a choice*, Doom said. *He chose her.*

She turned the radio to NPR and forced herself to focus on
the voices. She hated feeling like this, twitchy and jealous and
stupid. Yes, she felt stupid. Here she was heading for her first

ever girls' day out to shop for a wedding gown while her fiancé got together with his ex.

*Stupid.* She either trusted him or she didn't. She always had before. This engagement thing suddenly felt like too much pressure. How could anyone hold up under all that heavy expectation? If only there were clear-cut simple rules to follow to ensure a happy future. She thrived in environments where she understood the boundaries and rules. That was the way she'd been raised. And that was the way of physics.

She switched the radio to a hard rock station and blasted it. She needed to get out of her head on this three-hour drive or she'd never be able to deal with her mother. That always required maximum effort. Her mom pushed all her buttons, especially since she'd fallen in love with Ian. Not being able to say "I love you" to Ian in the beginning of their relationship like a normal person made her realize her upbringing had been abnormally cold. She'd finally broken through that emotional barrier after Ian had been hospitalized as a result of her bad cooking (food poisoning from undercooked turkey). Seeing him unconscious in the ambulance had pushed the love words right out of her mouth.

Words she'd never, ever heard from her own mom. Or dad. Dammit. Why had she let Amber invite her mom?

By the time Kate parked in the well-to-do town of Greenport, Connecticut, where they'd be meeting for lunch followed by shopping at the nearby bridal boutiques, she was a little on edge. Okay, a lot.

She located Le Jardin, the nice French restaurant where her sister had made reservations, and went inside. Amber waved to her from where the women were already seated at a square table with a white tablecloth. She took her place next to Amber, who, being the fabulous older sister she was, immediately poured Kate a glass of chilled chardonnay and filled her in on the conversation.

Half a glass of wine later, her mind wandered. *So here I am being a bride.* The women were talking about Violet and the preschools that Amber was looking into for the fall. Her mom, a petite woman with severely short gray hair, wire-framed glasses, and sharp elf-like features, sat across from her. Kate supposed she was fortunate to have some of her dad's softer features. She had her mom's sharp cheekbones and small upturned nose but her dad's full lips and rounded chin. Next to her mom was her mother-in-law-to-be Susan. Kate suddenly wished Ian was with them. He was so good at making conversation fun, always teasing and making funny little jokes. People often thought because she had a serious demeanor that they had to speak to her in a serious way, but she really appreciated when they didn't because it was nice to have a break from herself.

She finished her wine on a near empty stomach, which had the pleasant effect of shoving the impending sense of doom off a cliff. She smiled to herself. The cure for all relationship worries! Silly chimp. She bit back a giggle at her own monkey joke. And then Susan surprised her.

"Look at us gabbing on and on about Violet when it's Kate's special day," Susan said, smiling kindly at Kate. "Let's order some champagne and have a toast."

"Great idea!" Amber said, flagging the waitress down. So far they'd only had bread and a first course of salad.

"Thank you, Susan," Kate said. "That's kind of you."

Susan's warm brown eyes gazed at her lovingly. So much like Ian's. He was so lucky to have a mom with warm loving eyes. "You're family now."

Her mom, Maxine, spoke up in her tight clipped voice. "Technically Kate isn't family until after the marriage certificate has been filed at the courthouse. Kate, will you be keeping your last name? I strongly suggest it for professional reasons."

"Yes, I'll be keeping Lewis," Kate replied. "I figured for our kids we'd do the hyphenated last name like Amber and Barry did to avoid confusion."

"Lewis-Furnukle is a mouthful," her mom stated.

"We do okay with it," Amber said.

"I kept my maiden name," Susan said. "I quite agree Furnukle is a mouthful."

Amber giggled, and Kate snorted, fighting back a laugh. Her sister was *so* inappropriate. *Ha-ha-ha.*

"Whatever you're comfortable with, sweetheart," Susan added.

*I can take the whole Furnukle.*

"Thank you," Kate said with a straight face. Amber was still grinning. Kate kept her eyes on Susan and not her giggly sister. She didn't want her mother-in-law to think she was always taking a mouthful of her son's Furnukle. Even if she did on a regular basis. She felt herself flush remembering the last time. Ian gripping her hair, telling her he was going to fuck her mouth. Such a dirty talker. She pressed her cold water glass to her forehead.

Thankfully, a few minutes later the champagne arrived, and the waiter poured them each a glass.

"To Kate and Ian," Susan said, raising her glass.

"To Kate and Ian," the women chorused. Kate held her glass, unsure what to say.

They clinked glasses and drank. Kate relaxed more than she ever thought possible with her mom around.

Her mom wrinkled her nose. "I never did care for champagne." Kate took another drink of champagne like the rebel she never was. "Kate, your father and I would like to offer you a large sum of money toward a down payment on a house or toward the wedding. Your choice."

Kate nearly choked on her champagne. She hadn't expected her parents to do anything beyond show up at the appointed time for the wedding.

"I recommend the house option," her mom said. "In case of divorce you'll still come out ahead. Fifty percent of marriages end in divorce."

"Maxine!" Amber chided. "This is a celebration."

Kate put her hand up. "I'm well aware of the statistics and literature on marriage outcomes, Mom."

"Excellent," her mom said. "I wish I'd been so knowledgeable before my early marriages. I also wish I had kept my name."

"What? Your what?" Kate exclaimed. "I thought you were only with dad."

Amber looked surprised too. Susan discreetly sipped her champagne.

Her mom retrieved a soft lens cleaning cloth from the pocket of her tailored pants, took off her glasses, and cleaned them industriously. She blinked, her blue eyes softer now when they met Kate's across the table. "I was married twice before your dad."

Kate's jaw dropped. She did a quick calculation. Her mom was thirty-five when she had Kate. For two failed marriages before that, she must've started young. "Who? How long were you married? How old were you?"

"I was twenty-two and twenty-six," her mom replied, answering only the last question. She slid her glasses back on. "I learned the hard way that you want a work partner for a successful relationship. Neither of my exes respected my career as a physicist."

"Holy crap," Amber said.

"Did you love those other men?" Kate asked.

Her mom cleared her throat before confiding, "Yes."

"But what happened? Why did those first two marriages fail and the one with dad stuck?" She gripped her hands together tightly, both fearing the answer and needing to know. Because Kate was, unfortunately, a lot like her mom.

Her mom sighed. "If you must know, those first two marriages were all sizzle and heat." She leaned across the table. "Kate, do you understand my subtle meaning?"

"Yes," she whispered. Sex. Her mom had rowdy sex relationships. She shuddered at the thought.

Unfortunately that was exactly what she had with Ian.

Doom pulled out a chair and took a seat.

Her eyes darted around the table. Amber and Susan averted their eyes in polite silence.

Her mom went on. "Your dad was also a physicist working at the same university. We're work partners, as I said. Our marriage has always been a meeting of minds. I wish the same for you."

She felt light-headed. The quiet, cold home life of her childhood made perfect sense now. Her mom's marriage that worked wasn't a passionate love match, but rather an intellectual merger. Her parents probably only had sex the one time necessary to conceive her!

Was her passionate love match going to fall apart? Had she calculated incorrectly?

Dammit! She hadn't calculated at all!

"In any case," her mom went on, "we've saved for this occasion and are willing to pay for your first house or first marriage. Since you went to Princeton for undergrad, we were able to save considerably on college tuition." Kate had attended undergrad tuition-free since her parents were both professors there. Even in grad school she'd had a partial scholarship.

*Your first marriage*, Doom whispered in her ear, sounding exactly like her mother. The words echoed through her head, taunting her. Her mom had been divorced twice. Her dad had been divorced once. Kate had bad genes and a bad background. And poor Ian came from a stable loving family. Why in the world would he want a bad luck woman like her?

She broke out in a sweat and guzzled her champagne and then her ice water too for good measure.

The food arrived and Kate stared at her plate of rosemary chicken, all appetite gone.

Finally Susan piped up in an overly enthusiastic voice. "Kate, I would love to help pay for the wedding so you and Ian will have a special day. Then you can use your mom's generous gift for a house."

"You don't have to do that," Kate said. Susan was a widow on a fixed income.

"I have some life insurance money," Susan said. "Barry had money of his own for his wedding, who the heck knows when Daniel will ever settle down, so that leaves Ian. Please don't stop me from spoiling my youngest son!" Daniel was the middle son, a soldier, now in military intelligence. He never even dated. Just hookups. Ian had told her all about it when she'd first met Daniel at Barry and Amber's wedding and thought he was hot. Still.

"I don't know," Kate said.

"It's what his dad would've wanted," Susan said quietly. There was no way to say no to that. Kate had never met Ian's dad, but his death six years ago had been a difficult loss for all of their family. Susan had been very close with her husband.

Kate swallowed hard. "Of course, thank you."

Her mom spoke up. "It's settled, then. Now we need to nail down the logistics for the engagement party."

Everyone started eating and chatting about the engagement party that Susan, Amber, and apparently her mom were planning for them, but Kate found she couldn't even smile. Her gut was churning, her mind was total chaos, and her heart hurt.

Because now she had cold feet.

Kate had thought the wedding gown shopping would be a quick trip. She already had a picture of the gown she wanted on her cell phone—a strapless poufy dress of tulle with a lace bodice and a cute bow at the waist. She had the needed breast size to hold it up. No veil, just a tiara. She'd found the gown online for the bargain price of one hundred twenty-five dollars. She figured she'd just show the clerk what she wanted and wait for them to bring it or special order it.

Unfortunately, the beautiful bridal boutique where they headed right after lunch didn't have the gown Kate wanted. She took that as a very bad sign. That, in itself, was a very bad sign because Kate didn't believe in bad signs. She could feel herself losing it as one bad sign piled on top of another. The upscale boutique had at least fifty gowns in the petite section, none of them under five hundred dollars. She was about to hyperventilate. Not only was this her first marriage, it was her first time spending a lot of money. Other people's money, which made it much worse. What if things didn't work out?

What if everyone paid for all this wedding and engagement stuff and it was only for one day, one big party, that might be her last wedding or might be her first of many.

Maybe she was doomed by her mom's prediction. Ian wasn't a work partner at all. And that was the marriage that stuck for her mom. Ian had no clue what she worked on, though he nodded and smiled at the appropriate intervals. *Pant. Pant.* She was hyperventilating. Her first panic attack couldn't be far off. *Pant. Pant.* She'd read about panic attacks in brides who were engaged to the wrong men. *Pant. Pant.*

She bolted outside and sucked in air.

Amber appeared at her side a moment later. "Are you okay?"

Kate's mouth felt tight. Like she had her mom's tight clipped voice through tight lips. She was turning into her mom already! *Breathe, dammit!*

Amber put a hand on her arm. "Kate?"

Kate took a deep breath in and out. She heard her own clipped voice as if from some distance and listened like a horrified bystander. "I'm uncomfortable with the price tags on these gowns." And many other uncomfortable things she didn't dare voice lest she give them power and they destroyed everything! *Breathe!*

Amber hugged her. "It's okay. Maxine says she wants to buy it for you. It's a gift from her and Dad since you're their only daughter."

Kate stiffened, returning to herself at this terribly inaccurate statement. "That's wrong. You're their daughter too. Did they pay for your wedding gown?" Amber was her half-sister, true, but they had the same dad and had lived together since Kate was six and Amber was thirteen. They. Were. Family.

Amber smiled. "No, but I have a rich husband." This was true. Barry's Giggle Snap app had been a windfall. Somehow Amber got the rich genius husband and Kate got the charmer. Not how she would've guessed things would go with Amber being the free-spirited artist and Kate being a scientist. *Pant. Pant.* Things were all askew. What if they switched brothers?

Her brain got even more squirrely from there, frantically trying to outrun her anxiety with reasonable platitudes. Ian was wonderful. She was awful. Ian wasn't here. She didn't want to be here.

She was doomed and dragging Ian down with her!

Everyone was going to go broke on this wedding that might or might not have been a huge mistake!

She never should've proposed!

"Kate," Amber said gently, "you look a little pale."

*Breathe!*

Kate took another deep breath in and out. When she finally spoke, her voice came out sounding like her mom despite an effort to sound normal. "I prefer to order the inexpensive gown online." At least no one would go broke on her messed-up self.

"Are you upset about something?" Amber asked.

"I wish Ian were here," she muttered.

"Aww, you guys are so cute. I love seeing you in love. Come on, I'll help you pick. I know what you like with all the puffy gowns. We'll find something together."

"Let's do something crazy," Kate said because she really didn't want to go back in there and hyperventilate again, which would inevitably lead to a panic attack, proving she was a bride engaged to the wrong man.

Amber grinned. "Hit me."

Kate smacked her arm.

"Ow! You dope." Amber gave her a little smack back on the arm. "I didn't mean literally."

"Oh."

"Hit me with your best crazy idea."

"I would like a piercing." The idea was the craziest thing she could think of at the moment, considering she hated needles.

"Where?"

Kate pointed to her earlobes. "I've never had earrings."

"You would look so cute with earrings! Especially if your hair's up, we can get some crystal drop earrings that would look wonderful with your dream bridal tiara."

"Or just for every day," Kate said. "Except for in the lab."

Amber pushed Kate's hair over her ear. "Perfect. You can take them in and out whenever you want. Switch them up. They won't get in your way like a bracelet or necklace."

"Does it hurt?" Kate belatedly asked. Not that it mattered. Anything to avoid the carousel of horror—panic attacks, wasted money, her mother—awaiting her in the bridal boutique. Her mom was now standing very close to a mirror in the middle of the shop, staring herself down. This odd behavior seemed a very bad sign on top of a huge pile of bad signs.

"Piece of cake," Amber replied. "We'll do that after the manicure. Let's go try on gowns."

"Manicure? How long is this day?" Kate blurted. At Amber's annoyed look, she quickly amended, "I mean, how many things do you have planned?"

"It's a surprise. Now just relax and enjoy."

Kate dug her heels in. "Relax and enjoy" was not in her DNA, and the alcohol had worn off enough to remind her of that. She blurted the first thing she could think of to distract her sister. "Perhaps a tattoo would also be a good idea. I could wear that in the lab."

Amber narrowed her eyes. "You want a tattoo? You? You pass out every time you get a needle."

Kate looked through the front window of the boutique, saw her mom pacing back and forth, and for some reason that just wound her tighter. "Yes."

"What kind?" Amber asked.

"Big and colorful," Kate replied. "The kind that takes seven hours or more."

"Seven hours, huh?"

"Or more." Why was her mom pacing? Did she know the marriage was doomed?

"And what would you get?"

"Hopefully not hepatitis C or any other communicable disease."

"I meant what design," Amber said dryly.

Kate turned back to her sister. "I'll ask the artist to surprise me."

Amber pulled out her cell and punched a few buttons. She handed the phone to Kate. "Talk."

"Hello," Kate said. "Who's this?"

"It's me," Ian said.

His deep voice soothed her immediately. "Hi," she said, turning her back on Amber for privacy.

"Why'd you call in the middle of your girls' day out?" Ian asked.

"I didn't call. Amber did."

"Put Amber on."

She handed the phone back to Amber, who said, "We're at the bridal boutique. She's freaking out, talk her down," and handed back the phone.

"What's wrong?" Ian asked.

Kate shot her sister a dark look. "I'm not freaking out. Amber is high on big-sister ego."

Amber laughed heartily and went back inside the boutique.

"How was lunch?" Ian asked.

"How was Morgan?" she snapped. "Sorry." She really shouldn't be talking to Ian in her current state. He couldn't help it if Docm, aka her mother, had taken over her brain.

She suddenly realized the women, including the sales-clerk, were all watching her curiously from inside the boutique. *Nothing to see here, ladies! Just a doomed bride chatting with her equally doomed groom!*

"She's fine," Ian said calmly. "We finished work hours ago." He sounded so normal it pulled her back from the crazy edge. "Did you have a good lunch?"

She turned away from the front window and all the curious eyes. "I had rosemary chicken."

"Uh-huh. How's the gown shopping going?"

"They don't have my preferred gown."

"Your mom doing a number on you?"

"If by number you mean is she making me tense, then yes. But that's always the case."

"Why are you freaking out?" he asked gently.

She blinked, her eyes hot, her throat tight.

"Kate," he prompted.

"I'm afraid I'm turning into my mother," she whispered.

"Impossible. You're not a shape-shifter."

She choked on a laugh and wiped her eyes. "I'm afraid you don't know what you're getting with me."

"Believe me, I know."

She wasn't sure if that was good or bad. He'd said she was difficult to live with. She stepped further away from the shop and whispered, "I just found out my mom was divorced twice before my dad."

"So?"

"She said they were passionate love matches and that's why they didn't work out."

"They were probably losers."

"Oh." For some reason, she hadn't considered that. But then she remembered her dad and their working relationship. "The marriage that stuck was a meeting of minds."

"Why are you telling me this?"

She hated to admit it, but Ian had a right to know. "I come from bad genes."

"Poor thing, beautiful, smart, and sexy. So horrible."

She shook her head, though he couldn't see her. Ian was terribly biased. "I almost hyperventilated from cold feet."

"I'll warm them up next time I see you."

Ian had an answer for everything, it seemed. But did he realize this could possibly be her first marriage and that could mean a lot of money down the drain for both their families? She was afraid to say the words "first marriage," which even now made her queasy. They were stuck in her head like a horrible song sung by her mother.

"What else?" he asked.

"We're a passionate love match. Not a meeting of minds."

"Works for me."

"Oh."

"Though I'd argue that we do meet in a truly mental place on occasion. Sadly, it's true we're mostly about sex."

She could hear the smile in his voice. "You're teasing."

"You're not your mother."

She really wanted that to be true. Of course, intellectually she understood she wasn't her mother, but the similarities and her family history did give her pause.

"My mom wants to buy me a really expensive gown," she said, subtly touching on the first-marriage big-expense problem. "Even though it's just for one day."

"You wouldn't be Cinderella if it was for more than one day. Let her go nuts."

"Yeah?"

"If she offered, let her. Geez, Kate, when has she ever bought you a dress?"

Never. He was right. She'd never been allowed to wear dresses as a kid. Wow. This was kinda weird now that she thought about it.

"Isn't it strange that she wants to?" she asked.

"Maybe she realized it was about damn time."

"Ian," she said slowly, "did you talk to her about this ahead of time?"

"Will you be mad if I did?"

She gasped. "I can't believe you!"

"Love you too. Now go buy a pretty dress." He hung up.

She stood there for a long moment, a little dazed, her heart full of amazed wonder at the way Ian looked out for her. He must've called her mom this morning when Kate was on the road with Doom. While she was busy freaking out about their relationship and what it meant that he wasn't with her this weekend, he'd been making sure she had a good time. Her bad luck genes didn't faze him at all. Not even her cold feet made him waver.

She squared her shoulders and returned to the boutique.

The women hustled her into a dressing room where gowns were already waiting for her to try on. She peeked her head out. "Amber?"

Amber rushed over. "Yes?"

"Can you find me a tiara too?"

"You got it!"

Kate stripped down and put on the first satin and tulle beauty. Wow. Lace, beading, so much poofiness. She pulled her bun out and redid her hair in a high ponytail, twisted the end, and tucked it into the hair band for the full updo effect.

She stepped out into the boutique, where Amber, Susan, and her mom were sitting on a long white sofa.

"It's lovely," Susan said.

"Gorgeous," Amber said.

"My girl is all grown up!" her mom cried and broke down in sobbing tears.

Kate stared, horrified. She'd never seen her mom cry. Ever. "Mom?"

**14**

---

Kate's mom sobbed into Susan's shoulder. Kate exchanged a horrified look with Amber. Whoa.

She crossed to her mom and looked down at her crumpled form. "You must know I was grown up before I put on a wedding gown. I'm not sure why you're crying now. Why not cry when I graduated high school? Or moved out of the house? Or moved cross country?"

Her mom lifted her head, her glasses crooked. "I cried those times too!"

"But you seemed so serious and unemotional," Kate said.

"I was holding it together for your sake," her mom said. "I wanted you to have a strong female role model." She turned to Susan. "I need a tissue." Susan fished one out of her purse, and her mom took off her glasses and wiped her eyes with the tissue.

Mind blown.

Kate looked to Amber, who was looking at her mom with concern. Her world was askew again. She was standing in a beautiful white wedding gown, watching her mom fall apart. Not at all the cold formal woman Kate knew. She did a quick self check-in Her breathing remained normal, which told her she was indeed marrying the right man. The tension was simply from the sudden change of perspective. She didn't know what to do with this new information.

Amber shifted to sit next to Kate's mom, hugged her, and gestured for Kate to do the same. Kate switched places with Amber and hugged her mom—a new experience for both of them.

Kate patted her back awkwardly. "There, there. I'm going to be a grown-up for some time."

Her mom let out a weird half-laugh, half-sob.

"You can still be strong and have feelings too," Kate said. "I would've admired that as well."

"I just…" Her mom sniffled and blew her nose. "I wanted nothing to stand in your way. I wanted you to stand tall with the other physicists. I knew what you'd be up against being in the female minority."

"You taught me to work hard," Kate said, "which has been a great benefit. The men I work with have been quite pleasant."

"I'm very glad to hear it," her mom replied, sounding more like her old self. "Perhaps this younger generation isn't as sexist."

Kate had never thought about things being difficult for her mom. She always seemed determined, confident, and enthusiastic about her work. What had it cost her to project that image for so long? Both at work and at home. "Thank you for your valiant efforts on my behalf," Kate said. "But, uh, new rule. From now on, you can express yourself fully with your adult daughter and we will commiserate together."

"I'd like that," her mom said softly.

Kate looked over to Amber, who was quietly wiping tears. "Excuse me, Amber needs a hug."

Kate hugged Amber and then, for good measure, Susan, who was smiling, but she didn't want her new mother-in-law to be left out of the hug fest.

"Okay," Kate announced. "Now everyone help me pick out a good gown for my first wedding."

"And your last!" Amber and Susan said at the same time.

Her mom gave her a watery smile. "I hope so. I'm sorry I set a bad example with my failed marriages."

"They're certainly no reflection on you," Kate said magnanimously, even though she knew better than anyone that her mom was difficult to live with. She whirled in her gown, making the bottom spin and fly out, and went to try on more expensive gowns, for her first ever mother-daughter dress time.

Hours later, Kate had tried on every variation of gown—poufy ones, twirly ones, slinky ones, mermaid-style weird-ness—and settled on the first one. "Guess we could've saved a lot of time if I'd stuck with my first instinct," she said. "Sorry you had to wait around for that."

"Don't be silly!" Amber exclaimed. "We had fun. Anyway, I knew it would take a while. We still have half an hour before we get our nails done. Let's stop for ice cream on the way."

"Sounds good to me," Susan said.

"Ice cream is a soothing balm to the soul," her mom said.

Kate's jaw dropped. "Mom, that was so poetic."

"There's a beautiful poetry to the universe," her mom said. "I just choose to describe it with mathematical equations."

"Me too!" Kate exclaimed.

"Two peas in a pod," Amber muttered. And, for once, Kate didn't mind the comparison.

They had ice cream and talked about the food Kate would like at the engagement party. She wanted a variety of savory and sweet items that would appeal to everyone. Kate was also surprised to hear it would be at the Jorge Chavez Dance Studio. Amber had arranged for them to have ballroom dance lessons followed by a buffet style of food and dancing for anyone who wanted to hit the dance floor. Another piece of her Cinderella fantasy was settling into place. She had the gown, she had the prince, and now she'd have the elegant waltz.

Finally Kate settled in for her first ever manicure. "I'd like pink with violet flowers for my niece," she told the woman.

"I'll have the same," her mom said. "Violet is my grandchild."

They settled side by side. Amber and Susan were across from them. Amber was getting violet to match the violet streaks in her blond hair. Susan was getting an elegant plum color. Lot of purple going on for the Violet fan club.

"You still up for getting your ears pierced?" Amber asked Kate.

Her mom turned to her. "You know you pass out with needles."

"Amber says it's not that bad," Kate said. "Right? Piece of cake?"

"They don't use needles," Amber said, not quite confirming the piece-of-cake part. "It's like a little nail gun."

Kate's stomach rolled. "A nail gun on my ear?" She wanted to cover her ears protectively, but her nails were still being done.

"It's not as painful as childbirth," Susan said frankly. "And if you want drugs for that, there's going to be a long-ass needle in your spine."

"In my spine!" Kate screeched.

Amber smiled serenely. "I had natural childbirth with Violet. Hurt like a mo-fo, but it's worth it. In fact, we're trying for baby number two."

"Wonderful!" Susan exclaimed.

"Another grandchild," her mom said on a happy sigh.

"Are you crazy?" Kate barked at her sister. "You're voluntarily signing up for 'hurt like a mo-fo' pain again?"

Amber nodded and smiled.

"I will *not* be getting my ears pierced," Kate announced. "I refuse to sign up for voluntary pain when there is mo-fo pain or possible long-ass needles in my future."

"But the crystal drop earrings will look so good with your tiara," Amber said.

Kate hesitated. Earlier Amber had shown Kate some delicate gorgeous crystal earrings she'd found online. Damn. She wanted those earrings badly. They were perfect and would highlight the crystals in her tiara. On the other hand, she was a wimp.

The nice woman doing Kate's nails looked up. "We can pierce your ears here if you want. Shanna does them. Only hurts for a minute."

Her mom turned to her. "I'll get mine pierced too. I let them close up thirty years ago. Then we can be earring twins."

A mother-daughter ear piercing? How feminine! How rite of passage! How female solidarity reveling in body art togethering!

Kate swallowed hard. "Okay, but you go first."

"That's fine," her mom said. "I'm tough."

The gauntlet was laid down.

"The Lewis women are all tough!" Amber exclaimed.

"Yeah! The Dancy women too," Susan said in a tough-guy voice. Dancy was her maiden name.

That was it. There was no way Kate could be a wimp surrounded by all these strong women.

Once their nails were done, and hers turned out quite stunning, she followed her mom to a chair in the back where an ear-piercing station was set up. Shanna waited nearby, looking tough with her hair shaved on one side and a dozen earrings lining her earlobe on both sides as well as a nose piercing, eyebrow piercing, and lip piercing. *Ow, ow, ow, ow.*

Kate watched her mom climb up on the high swivel chair, looking her usual calm and composed self.

Shanna pulled out a display of starter earrings on a black velvet tray. "What would you like?"

Kate leaned closer to look. There were gold balls, silver balls, tiny rhinestones, hearts, stars, moons, and a variety of other geometric shapes. So cute. She already knew she wanted stars.

"You pick," her mom said to Kate.

"Stars," she said.

"Stars it is," her mom pronounced. Wow. They really were going to be earring twins. If Kate didn't chicken out. She'd wait and see if her mom winced or screamed or leaped out of her seat. Any of which Kate would do. If she didn't pass out.

Amber and Susan watched from nearby. Amber had her cell phone up, snapping pictures. "You think Dad will like it?" Amber asked Maxine.

Her mom turned. "I will like it and that's what matters." Total badass mom.

Shanna pulled out the piercing tool, which did look like a nail gun, only much smaller, and loaded it. Then she cleaned her mom's ears with an alcohol wipe. Kate broke out in a sweat.

Her mom watched in a small mirror as Shanna lined up the first earlobe. *Pop!* Kate jumped, but her mom remained impassive, still watching in the mirror. Shanna did the other ear. *Pop!* Kate cringed.

"What do you think?" Shanna asked.

Her mom tilted her head, looking in the mirror. "I like it."

Her mom got up and stood to the side. Kate stared at the empty chair.

"Go ahead, Kate," Susan said. "You can do it."

Amber held up her cell phone with the picture of the crystal drop earrings Kate coveted.

"Would you like me to hold your hand?" her mom asked.

Kate flushed. Her mom had held her hand for every shot she'd ever gotten. And she still passed out. She didn't want to look like a giant baby. She was an adult about to embark on the very adult journey of marriage and children.

"Yes," she said.

She took the seat, and her mom held her hand. Amber got close to video the whole thing. Now she really couldn't look like a wimp. Amber would show Barry and possibly Violet this video. She had to be a strong female role model for Violet. Besides, if Ian heard she passed out, he'd tease her relentlessly. He'd had an earring in college. Surely if Ian could do this, she could. Were men tougher than women? No. Did men push giant baby heads out of a tiny hole? No. Did she want those crystal drop earrings that complimented her tiara and gown perfectly? Yes.

Shanna touched her earlobe with something cold, and Kate jumped. "That was just the wipe," Shanna said.

Kate squeezed her mom's hand as she always did when a needle was about to get close.

"Katherine, perhaps it's time we have a frank talk about the secret of men," her mom said in her formal tone.

"Mom, we've had the birds and bees talk many times," Kate said. "I'm good. Is there some other secret about men I need to know?" Kate's mind whirled with possibilities—this secret could have to do with her dad, in which case, she wasn't so sure she wanted to know. "Does this have to do with a particular man or men in general? Ow!"

"First star in," her mom said. "Take a look."

Her ear burned. She couldn't look. Oh God. She didn't think she could take another pop and burn.

"It's about your dad," her mom said.

"What about Dad?" Kate asked. This better not be sexual. Geez, she had to have a talk about boundaries with her mom if she thought this new mother-daughter bonding stuff included hearing sex stuff about her dad. "Ow!"

"All done!" her mom exclaimed.

"You did it!" Amber cried.

"How do you feel?" Susan asked.

*Pant. Pant. Pant.*

"You were so brave," Amber said. "Wait until Violet sees. She's going to want some earrings too."

Kate took a deep breath and looked in the mirror. Her mom's face appeared next to her. "Earring twins," her mom said. "Awesome."

Kate smiled at the word her mom had never uttered before with her. "Awesome," Kate echoed.

They left, Kate feeling bonded and badass for not passing out, when a thought occurred to her. "What were you going to tell me about Dad?"

"That was a classic misdirection ploy," her mom said. "You've always fallen for those when you got a needle."

"But I didn't pass out this time," Kate said proudly.

"I should hope not. Ear piercing is a minor event compared to a vaccine."

Kate felt a little less badass then.

"But for you a major event," her mom hastily amended. "And a first in the mother-daughter events to come."

"What's next?" she couldn't help but ask.

"I'll hold your hand during childbirth."

"Who held your hand?"

"No one. I'm tough."

"Oh, I guess I'm not that tough."

Her mom squeezed her hand. "You're strong. Enough to lean on someone when you need it and handle it yourself when you don't. I greatly admire that."

She had to force the words out over the lump in her throat. "Thanks, Mom." Her mom had never admired her for anything besides her academic work before.

After that they went shoe shopping. By the time they got back to Barry and Amber's place, Kate was exhausted. She stepped inside and did a double take.

"Ian! What are you doing here?" she exclaimed. "How did you get here?" She'd taken his car.

He grinned and opened his arms to her. "Surprise! I took the train."

She felt her cheeks flush. She wasn't so good at surprises, but she was very happy to see him after this emotional day. She rushed into his arms.

"We got the gown and came home with earring twins!" Amber exclaimed, gesturing to Kate and her mom. "Wait until you see the video of Kate getting her ears pierced."

Barry and Ian wore identical looks of surprise, but recovered quickly. "Very nice," Barry said.

"Both Drs. Lewis look beautiful," Ian said, settling an arm around her shoulders.

"Please call me Maxine," her mom said. "We'll be family soon."

"Okay, Maxine," Ian said warmly.

"Stars!" Violet exclaimed with her cute lisp.

"Violet, you have to wait until you're twelve before you

get earrings," Barry pronounced.

"That's an arbitrary number," Kate said. "Unless you're using it as a rite of passage into womanhood and in that case—"

"We'll discuss it," Amber said.

Ian kissed Kate and then pushed her hair back to look at her ear. "Don't touch," she said. "It burns."

"It is red," he said. "What made you want to be earring twins with your mom?"

"It's a mother-daughter thing," she said.

Her mom beamed.

Ian grinned. "All right, then."

"You want to see Kate's video?" Amber asked. Everyone gathered close to watch on Amber's cell phone screen. Even Kate watched. It looked like piercing was no big deal from the outside. You couldn't even hear the pop of the piercing tool with her mom distracting her and Kate wondering what the hell her mom was talking about. She didn't look as badass as she'd felt after. Bummer. Maybe she'd look badass giving birth. They'd need a video of that too.

A short while later, Barry cooked them a delicious dinner on the grill. Her mom left after that, even stopping to give Kate a hug in a nice goodbye. The house was quiet once Amber took Violet upstairs for her bath and bed routine. Barry headed out back to clean the grill.

Ian grabbed her hand and led her to the dining room. He pulled out a chair for her and took the chair across the table, saying, "Let's talk."

Since they were alone, she had to ask, "Did you come here because I had cold feet?"

One corner of his mouth lifted in his crooked smile. "Actually, approximately ten minutes into my work meeting, I realized I was being a complete idiot to waste one moment of our time together. I booked it out of there, bought a train ticket, and headed down to my girl."

Her heart filled to bursting. She found herself grinning like a fool.

His warm brown eyes met hers. "And I'll be working part-time from home this week so we can spend more time together."

"Perfect!"

He pulled out his cell and tapped it. "I brought my bug report. We're going to go through both reports and hammer out the details that matter in this relationship. Because you matter."

"Oh, Ian!" she exclaimed, pulling out her cell. "That would be wonderful. Let me get Barry. It's important to have an impartial third party to facilitate these things. It's in all the literature." She leaped up.

"Is that really necessary?" he asked.

She slowly sat down again. "No, I guess not. Let me just, uh, look it over first." She wasn't so sure he'd like some of the stuff in her report, and she didn't want him to get mad again after he travelled all this way to see her.

Kate was still pretending to review her bug report, working up the nerve to show Ian, when Barry unexpectedly joined them, plopping down in the seat at the head of the table.

"Hey, lovebirds," Barry said, "texting each other?"

"Actually we're reviewing the bug reports you suggested we make," Kate said.

Barry waggled his brows comically. "Let me see what you got, Kate. This oughta be good."

She handed over her cell. Ian groaned.

Barry read and read and read. "Wow, Kate. A sixty-seven item list. How much is on your list, Ian?"

"Three things," Ian mumbled. It was like he wasn't paying any attention these past couple of weeks.

Barry handed back her cell and stood. "Good luck."

Kate worried her lower lip. Her sixty-seven item list to Ian's three item list might lead to some hostility. His.

She watched Barry's retreating back as he headed to the living room. "We don't need to do the bug report," Kate told Ian.

"I know it's important to you. What're you worried about?"

"I don't want you to get mad again. You came all this way."

Ian turned and called his brother back from the living room. Kate's eyes widened.

"You sure?" Barry asked, returning to the room.

"We'd like your impartial opinion," Ian said. "You'll be our software engineer working out the bugs."

Kate beamed at Ian for being so considerate. He jerked his chin at her in a gesture that wasn't happy, but said he was all in. Technically Barry would be their couples therapist, not an engineer. This seemed like the perfect way to ensure a positive outcome.

Barry went to the kitchen and returned with a pen and small notepad. He took his seat at the head of the table and steepled his fingers in front of him. "Where should we begin? With Kate's concerns or yours?"

"Might as well start with hers," Ian said. "She wrote a book."

"I'd hardly call a sixty-seven-item list a book!" Kate exclaimed, handing over her cell.

"First rule of communication," Barry said. "No one raises their voice. You're both too sensitive not to take offense. Then it escalates. Then—" he glanced down at Kate's report "—Ian uses a short circuit of some kind, which Kate has a problem with."

Ian dropped his head in his hands and groaned.

"Perhaps I should've been more explicit," Kate started.

Ian lifted his head. "Kate," he said sharply. Though she noticed he made an effort not to raise his voice.

She leaned across the table and lowered her voice. "What? You're supposed to share everything with your engineer."

"Not that," Ian bit out.

Barry chuckled. "I think I get the picture. So it seems one of Kate's main concerns is establishing a good communication system. I'm going to jot down a few rules for you both to follow. One, no one raises their voice. Two, no one uses a short circuit until both parties have agreed the issue is resolved. Okay?"

"Yes," Kate said.

"Ian?" Barry asked.

"Fine," Ian grumbled. She was extra happy with him for doing this despite his grumpiness about sharing with an impartial couples therapist, err, software engineer.

Barry wrote for a few moments and then smiled. "This is progressing nicely. Any other communication concerns?"

"No," Ian said.

Kate piped up. "I would like Ian to communicate exactly what he's willing to share in his apartment and what he won't share. He has a territoriality issue."

"I do *not* have a territoriality issue," Ian growled.

"Good job keeping your voice down," Kate said. He really was doing a nice job at that. It gave her hope that he'd take the rest of Barry's wisdom seriously.

"Ah, yes," Barry said. "I did read of these territoriality incidents with great interest. Some very detailed observations you made here, Kate."

Kate smoothed her hair. "Thank you. I do have nice attention to detail. It's a must as a physicist."

"Uh-huh," Barry said. "And is Ian a particle that you enjoy studying?"

She straightened. "Uh, no, of course not. He's the male."

"Hmm…" Barry said.

Ian stared at the ceiling.

Barry tapped his pen on the paper and looked at her. She squirmed. Was he waiting for her to come up with some solution to Ian's territoriality problem?

"Kate," Barry finally said, "forgetting Ian's issue for a moment, let's talk about you. What's your most important material possession?"

"My laptop," she replied immediately.

"And what if Ian found a sudden need to take your laptop to work with him and didn't check with you first? What if you woke up and it was just gone?"

She shot Ian a look. "Why would you take my laptop to work?"

Ian slowly shook his head.

"It's a hypothetical situation," Barry put in.

"I would be livid," Kate said. "There's no reason for that. He has his own laptop and plenty of computers at work. There's no reason to take my laptop with all my important work on it."

"So you might feel a little possessive about it?" Barry asked. "A little territorial?"

Kate sat for a moment, stunned. She was more than a little territorial about her laptop. On the other hand, there was no question her laptop was much more valuable than shaving cream. She felt compelled to state the quantitatively obvious. "Laptops are more valuable than shaving cream."

"What do you think, Ian?" Barry asked.

"It was pretty damn valuable to me that morning," Ian said. "I had a weekend's worth of scruff, three job applicants to interview at my new job, and no time to get more at the store."

"So in this special circumstance," Kate said, realization dawning, "the shaving cream *became* a valuable item."

"Excellent observation, Kate," Barry said. "I think it's safe to say that anyone can become territorial over an item that is much needed at that particular moment. So let's have a rule to ask the other person before taking their stuff, shall we?"

"Fine by me," Ian grumbled.

"That would be acceptable to me as well," Kate said. "Barry, please excuse my formal tone. This is a very emotional time for me and it's certainly not a reflection on your excellent engineering skills."

"You talk however you want," Barry said easily. He scribbled something quickly on the paper.

Kate relaxed a little, knowing they already had three rules. That was a great start.

"I really like having all these rules spelled out," Kate said. "Thank you."

Ian studied her across the table. "You like rules, Kate?"

"Yes."

"Maybe I'll come up with a few for you," he drawled.

"That would be most welcome," Kate replied enthusiastically.

"You'll have to follow them," Ian added. "Every single one."

"Of course," Kate replied. She caught his hot look across the table and felt her body heating in response, nipples tingling, a throbbing pulse between her legs. *Oh no.* She would *not* be short-circuiting at this important couples therapy session. She leaned across the table. "Stop that," she whispered fiercely.

"I'm not doing anything," Ian said, a sly smile crossing his expression.

She jabbed a finger at him and was about to say *stop that short-circuit business* when Barry interrupted.

"Okay, we have three very solid rules here that you're both willing to abide by. Now, I think the idea of his and hers labels might be counterproductive and encourage more territoriality. Might I suggest for certain items, you buy two?"

"Two milk cartons?" Kate asked.

"Yes, one for Ian to chug directly from," Barry said, shooting his brother a look of disgust, "and one for you to pour into a glass like a civilized person."

"That works for me!" Kate said happily. "I'll even buy a small jar of cashews. That way I can have just the nut I like and Ian can continue his random-handful-of-mixed-nuts obsession."

"It's not an obsession," Ian said.

Kate smiled to herself. Four very clear understandable rules. She felt better already.

Barry wrote quickly; then he set the pen down and leveled Kate with a serious look. "Kate, I fear you have a tendency to attribute traits to my brother that aren't there."

Ian smacked the table. "Thank you."

Kate took off her glasses and cleaned them industriously with the end of her shirt. She sensed an alliance of brothers and, without her sister here, she was sort of vulnerable. "How so?"

"Well, Ian's probably the most mellow, laid-back guy I know," Barry said. "Even more than me."

"That's one of the things that drew me to him," Kate said. "He made me feel relaxed."

"Good," Barry said. "I'm glad we're in agreement. So when you use words like *obsessed, territorial, hostile,* you can see how these labels might not exactly fit his true personality."

Kate shot Barry a dark look. Then she put her glasses back on and sent him a second dark look where she could actually see his expression. He looked kindly back at her. She huffed. "Those words were all warranted in those particular circumstances."

"Them's fighting words, Kate," Barry said.

Ian grunted.

"Another rule," Barry announced, picking up his pen with a flourish. "No labels, no name-calling, just stick to the facts."

Kate's eyes stung. This time the rule didn't make her feel better at all. She was the problem? She was screwing up the communication? She met Ian's eyes, and his return look was not angry or smug, but compassionate. She bit her lip.

Ian pushed his chair back from the table. "C'mere."

She stood and walked around the table to him. He hauled her into his lap so her back was to his front. She shifted slightly so he could hear her. "I'm sorry I screwed up our communication," she whispered. "I was putting it all on you. You were right, my report was biased. I wasn't a chimp I didn't know."

"It's okay," Ian said, wrapping his arms around her. He stroked her hair back from her face and kissed her cheek. She relaxed against him.

Barry smiled. "I think we're making excellent progress. Kate, will you be short-circuiting in Ian's lap, or can we continue?"

She felt too good to move. "We can continue."

Things went smoothly after that. Within a half hour, Barry had a list of six rules for an effective relationship (the sixth rule, added in response to Ian's complaints, her equations would remain untouched as long as she didn't use food or anything else perishable). Kate felt so good she even came up with a fair way of dividing the domestic chores—they made a list of the chores, and she and Ian took turns picking what they would be willing to do. Ideally they'd get a cleaning service like her parents had, but they didn't have the money for that.

They finished and Barry ripped off the piece of paper that was the key to a happy, harmonious future and handed it to Kate. She folded it neatly and tucked it into her purse.

"Thank you, Barry, for your patience and understanding," Kate said.

"Yeah, thanks, bro," Ian said. "That wasn't as bad as I thought."

"Anything for my two favorite people," Barry said, standing and stretching.

Kate went over and hugged her favorite brother-in-law in the whole world. Ian gave him a one-armed man hug too.

"I'm going to tell Violet goodnight," Barry said and headed upstairs.

Ian took her hand and walked with her to the living room. "You know how you said I'm the more nurturing of us two?" he asked once they were settled on the sofa.

"Yes."

"I don't think that's true anymore."

She jolted. Ian was always hugging her and giving her warm looks. It took her forever to be able to initiate a hug. Then she realized she had been hugging him and their family more. "Because of the hugs?"

"Yes, the hugs and the I love yous and expressing yourself without being overly formal. Though it sometimes slips out." He kissed the tip of her nose. "The way you adore Violet."

"Well, she is adorable."

"Maybe we could take turns taking care of our kids. I take some time off for the first kid, you take some time off for the second kid. What do you think?"

"Or maybe we both cut back hours and balance work shifts with kid shifts."

"Look how good we're doing already. Communicating, coming up with fair solutions to issues that everyone has."

"It's not just us," she said slowly. "There's nothing wrong with us." She gazed up at him. "This is all normal couple stuff. We're just a normal couple!"

"I wouldn't go that far, my little monkey." He leaned in for a kiss, and she slammed a hand on his chest.

"Wait. Before you short-circuit me—"

"The rule is short circuit allowed after issues resolved," he rumbled near her ear.

"I want to talk."

"Kiss and then talk." When she didn't kiss, he clenched his jaw. "Fine. What?"

"Thank you for talking to my mom about the wedding gown."

"You're welcome."

"What did you say?"

"I said, Dr. Lewis, this is the mother of all mother-daughter moments and it would mean a lot to Kate if you bought her a wedding gown. I also said I would pay for it if cost was an issue."

"And what'd she say?"

"She said, 'Thank you for your kind inquiry into this important occasion,' and then she hung up."

Kate cringed. "So you really didn't know if she'd do the mother-daughter thing or not."

"I knew she would."

Kate's brows scrunched together. "How did you know?"

"Because she got the formal tone you get when you're nervous or worked up about something. I knew it must mean something to her."

"She always sounds like that!"

His warm brown eyes gazed lovingly into hers, his mouth curving into a grin. "Give me some credit for understanding the way of the Lewis women."

She threw her arms around him and kissed him all over his face, and then she kissed his smiling mouth. He deepened the kiss, and she short-circuited, her mind shutting down, her body heating up. Everything would surely be smooth sailing from here on out. What could go wrong?

**15**

---

6 Rules for Ian-Kate Relationship

1. No one raises their voice.
2. No short circuit until both parties agree the issue is resolved.
3. Ask the other person before taking their stuff.
4. Keep >=2 items in stock of milk, nuts, and shaving cream.
5. No labels or name-calling, stick to the facts.
6. Equations allowed only on nonperishable items.

Ian was a little tense. Okay, a lot. But he wanted to prove he could do this rule-following thing that was so important to Kate. The rules were posted everywhere—above the toilet (clearly meant for those of us who stood to pee), on the bedroom door, on both of their nightstands, on the refrigerator, on the coffee table, and on the inside of the front door. He'd memorized them after the first day. Now, four days later, the rules just taunted him with their solid perfection. They hadn't fought once. They hadn't spontaneously made love once either because, of course, he had to check in if the issue was resolved before he could short-circuit her, which was his favorite thing to do, and by the time Kate ran down every possible path that would lead to an equitable solution to whatever the hell they had an "issue" about, he was nearly catatonic from her long-winded discussion and didn't have the energy.

Everything was perfectly harmonious, which should have been relaxing, but instead made him irritable. He wanted to shout at the top of his lungs *I hate rules!* Though he really wasn't that much of a rebel. He just liked things to be easy, sort of a go-with-the-flow kind of guy. Okay, yes, he'd been sneaking cashews from her special jar just to mess with her head. She kept puzzling over the nut level, wondering if she'd eaten more than she'd realized. And he hadn't said one word about her drinking from his supposedly unhygienic carton of milk instead of hers. That little victory made him happy.

He was a terrible person.

He looked across the kitchen table at Kate eating the dinner he'd prepared. Her expression was dreamy. Not from his cooking. She was thinking, looking off in the distance, instead of appreciating all his hard work. They'd followed the equitable division of chores list, which meant he'd cooked dinner all week. Mostly heating up frozen meals from the supermarket, like tonight's dish of lasagna, but he had boiled spaghetti all on his own and he always prepared a side dish of vegetables. And did Kate give one word of appreciation for all his effort in the kitchen? No. He'd washed and chopped and sautéed that broccoli. Did she even notice? No. She ate every meal like it was a necessary chore, excused herself, leaving all the dirty dishes in the sink (her chore), and took a long walk.

Sure, she put the dishes in the dishwasher later, and, by the way, she put everything in there, even stuff that had to be scrubbed by hand, which he later had to do, but…hell, dishes aside, if someone took the time to prepare a nice meal, then the other someone should mention if it was good or something.

She blinked and searched frantically for something to write with.

"Use the whiteboard on the fridge," he said before she could start writing with the lasagna sauce on the table. He'd bought the whiteboard special for her.

She leaped up and wrote something incomprehensible on the whiteboard with a lot of mathematical symbols. Then she returned to the table, standing to finish her glass of milk. Poured from his carton. *Muah-haha.*

"Did you like dinner?" he asked.

"Excellent, as always," she replied. "Thank you."

Now why didn't that make him feel better? He was so damn cranky ever since the rules had been posted.

She wiped her milk mustache with a napkin. "Would you like to take a walk with me?"

"No, thanks." He'd given up after the second night because she was impossible to talk to. The after-dinner walks were more like thinking tours for her brain. She frequently stopped to write notes on a small notepad from her purse. He could say, "It's raining penises," and she'd say, "Yes, very nice."

He stood.

"Are you finished?" she asked.

"Yeah."

"Perfect. I'll clear the two plates together." She stacked the plates and silverware, dumped them all in the sink, and headed for the door.

"Have fun," he said.

"See ya," she said absentmindedly and left.

With a herculean effort, he ignored the dirty dishes that were not on *his* list of chores, put away the leftover lasagna, and settled on the sofa to watch the Sox pregame. He was secretly glad his boss wanted him back at work full time next week. He couldn't take another harmonious week at home. He put his feet up on the coffee table and relaxed. The Sox were having a great season so far.

By the fourth inning, he was less relaxed. Kate had been gone a long time, much longer than her usual half hour, and it was starting to get dark. He worried about her wandering down some dark alley, oblivious to her surroundings. He snagged his cell to check the time. She'd been gone nearly two hours.

He called her. "Where are you?" he barked as soon as she answered.

"Almost home," she said.

"How far away?"

The front door opened. The relief at seeing her step through that door was overwhelming. He went to her and hugged her tight. He pulled away just enough to look at her. "Where were you?"

"I told you I was going for a walk."

"You were gone for two hours."

She cocked her head. "I was? I didn't realize. I had a lot of thinking to do."

He stroked her cheek. "What're you thinking so hard about?"

"I'm confused. I tried to do a self-check because I fear the problem is me, but the results have proven inconclusive." She bit her lip. "I mean, I'm still confused."

He took note of the formal tone, the confusion that probably affected him too, his own uneasy feeling coursing through him, and said the only thing he could say, "Okay, let's talk."

They settled side by side on the sofa. He grabbed the remote, turned down the volume, and turned to her. "What is it?"

She took off her glasses and cleaned them on the end of her T-shirt. Another tell of hers. She must be pretty worked up. "We've spent a lot of time together this week."

"Yeah, so?"

She frowned and slid her glasses back on. "We've both done an admirable job at following the relationship rules and the equitable distribution of chores."

"So what's the problem? I thought you liked rules."

She wrung her hands together. "I'm confused. We did everything right, yet I'm so restless. Like almost claustrophobic to be in the apartment with you, though I'm sure I still love you. What should I do?"

He knew exactly what to do. He grabbed the list of rules off the coffee table and ripped it into shreds.

Kate gasped. "Ian! What're you doing?"

"Fuck the rules," he said.

"Fuck the rules," she echoed, her blue eyes lighting with excitement.

"That's not us. You're restless because you like when we fight and yell and make up. You like when I short-circuit you whenever I damn well please. And so do I! All these rules were making me tense."

"You mean—" she smoothed her hair "—I'm secretly a rebel?"

He bit back a smile. "Definitely."

She looked thoughtful. While she was distracted, he pulled her hair band out and ran his fingers through the silky strands.

She turned to him with her excited eureka face. "There must be some kind of endorphin that kicks into my brain when we get worked up about something. You're such a worthy opponent, you know."

"Thanks," he said, lifting her hair and pressing a kiss to the side of her neck.

She shivered and kept talking, oblivious to his nefarious plan, too lost in her new discovery. "Like when you throw your dirty sock at the hamper and miss, and you just leave it there, balled up on the floor instead of putting it in. I haven't said a word about that all week because your job is laundry. So instead I ignored it and that irritation turned into apartment-sharing claustrophobia."

He slipped his hands under the back of her T-shirt to undo the bra clasp. "That's right, Kate. You need to get that stuff out." The bra sprang open, but she didn't notice, her eyes unfocused and dreamy. He rubbed her bare back. "Like when I made all those delicious dinners and you didn't say one word of appreciation until I asked you. That stuff makes a person tense."

"You mean *you* were tense while I was bored and restless," she said, focusing on him again. "Interesting."

"It is interesting," he told her, sliding off her glasses and setting them on the coffee table.

"I think the most interesting...*gurfle murfle muh.*" Her voice was muffled because he pulled her T-shirt up and over her head. He didn't ask her to repeat herself. Instead he tossed her shirt far away so she couldn't put it back on.

He skimmed his hand along the side of her neck. Her lips parted, cheeks flushed, but her eyebrows scrunched together like she was trying to concentrate. "Kate, do you know how badly I wanted to wipe that damn bathroom mirror clean of lipsticked equations?"

She licked her lips. "As badly as I wanted to confiscate the toothpaste tube until you learned how to use it properly?"

He slid her bra straps off her shoulders, pulled it off, and tossed that too. Then he cupped her breasts with both hands, stroking the tips that beaded with his touch.

"Did we resolve our issue?" she asked in a breathy voice.

"Who the fuck cares," he said before his lips met hers. She grabbed his head. He rolled on top of her, mouths fused together, and settled between her legs. He shifted to kiss along her jaw, lust driving him to move faster than he normally would. He sucked the cord of her neck, and she bucked underneath him. The rest was a hot blur, their hands grabbing frantically while they kissed passionately.

He stood and stripped out of his clothes, and she took his cue, yanking her shorts and panties off. Then he was on her, taking her in one swift thrust. She gasped and then urged him on, "Harder, faster, fuck, fuck, fuck." She was a talker, and he loved it. She lifted her legs higher, her heels digging into his back as he thrust deeper. He slid his hand under her ass, lifting her hips for the angle he needed. "Yes! Yes! Yes!" she shouted, and he just let go, pumping into her as she shuddered underneath him.

He stilled, buried deep inside her, breathing hard. He felt her shaking under him and lifted his head. She was quietly laughing.

"What's so damn funny?" he asked.

"I'm just happy," she said. "I never knew I was such a rebel."

He cupped her face with one hand and kissed her smiling mouth. "I love that about you." He went nose to nose with her, gazing into her bright blue eyes.

"I'm a badass too," she said. "Two piercings and I didn't pass out."

He'd never heard of someone passing out from getting their ears pierced. "I guess."

She smacked his shoulder. "What do you mean you guess? That is so badass. I usually pass out with needles."

"You do?"

"Yeah."

He kissed her. "Then I guess you're a badass."

"Think you can handle me?" she asked in a taunting voice.

He nipped her neck. "I'll handle you all right," he growled in her ear. Then he stood and carried her, cradled in his arms, to the bedroom. He tossed her on the bed. She landed with a bounce and a delighted laugh. "I'm gonna handle you until you break every rule."

"Do it," she said, revving him further.

"Manhandle, Kate." Then he grabbed her and handled her until he got her to raise her voice (rule one broken), completely short-circuit (rule two), take his stuff (rule three in a manner of speaking), share her high-value body (rule four, *aw, yeah*, his territory), call him every name she'd ever thought of, including some she hadn't (rule five, call me names, you dirty talker), and write equations all over his body in extremely perishable whipped cream (fuck rule six).

Fuck all the rules.

Kate woke early the next morning, lying naked on her stomach, which was where she'd collapsed after the third round with Ian. His stamina was incredible. He always wore her out long before he wore out. Probably because he wrung multiple orgasms out of her before taking his own single orgasm. Such a considerate alpha. How could he not have been the perfect ten to set the bar for all others?

She suddenly realized why she was awake. Her cell was ringing. She shifted and reached for it on the nightstand.

"Hello?" she whispered. No one there. It must've already went to voicemail. She shifted back next to Ian, lay on her stomach and propped up on her elbows, tapping her cell to check the voicemail.

A few moments later, she bolted upright in bed. "Ian!"

He groaned, still sleeping on his back. She set her cell on the nightstand and returned to Ian, shaking him by the shoulders. "Ian! Wake up!"

"Time is it?" he muttered.

"Wake up! I've got big news!"

No response. She straddled him and wiggled around a bit. She felt him grow hard under her; then his hands went to her hips, and his lips curved into a smile. "Mmm…" he said. His eyes were still closed.

She leaned forward and nipped his bottom lip to wake him up. Then she shrieked in surprise when he suddenly flipped her onto her back, pushing her legs apart with his body, his hands pinning hers to the mattress above her head.

"Morning, badass," he said, shifting his hips into position for what she knew would be a hard screw. He was an animal in the morning.

"Wait," she said. "I have to tell you some big news."

"After," he murmured, the words hot against the sensitive skin of her neck.

She moaned. Dammit! He was going to short-circuit her before she got to say her big news. She scrunched her eyes tight and focused the last of her brain power. "A weasel got into the Large Hadron Collider and now I've got it!" she said all in a rush.

He lifted his head, gazing at her for a long moment, his eyes still sleepy. "Got what?"

"It's mine!"

He stared at her blankly. "The weasel?"

"No, silly! The fellowship is mine! A weasel got into the Large Hadron Collider and ate through some power lines, shutting it down. Ha! Another short circuit in my favor! Since they couldn't work, the committee went through the fellowship applications ahead of schedule and I'm in! I got it!"

He released her hands and got off her, sitting next to her. She sprang up and threw her arms around him. "It's a dream come true!" she exclaimed.

He hugged her. "I'm so proud of you. Really good news. We'll celebrate once I'm more awake."

She bounced in place, her excitement needing an outlet. "I'm going to call Amber." She scooted to sit on the edge of the bed and grabbed her cell.

"Is Nate going with you?" Ian asked.

"Yes. Oh, good idea. I should call him too."

"I'll miss you."

She shifted to look at him. "What do you mean? I want you to come with me."

"I can't. My job is here."

"Tell them you want to work remotely."

"I worked remotely this week, and my boss didn't like it. The grad students need more hands-on supervision. That's the main reason they brought me on. I'm one of those rare people who understand the technology and have the social skills to manage a herd of nerds." He gave her a smile that looked forced. "Least that's what my boss said."

"Oh." She turned back to her cell, her excitement dimmed. And then Ian's heat was at her back.

He wrapped his arms around her waist, his legs on either side of hers. "I'll be right here when you get back."

She didn't say anything. This was not how she pictured things between them. Another year long distance? Even more long distance, across an entire ocean. "I thought you didn't want a long-distance marriage."

He brushed her hair back and kissed her temple. "I don't. We'll have a long-distance engagement."

Tears stung her eyes. She told herself to suck it up. It

wasn't like they were breaking up. She was engaged, for crying out loud.

Ian pulled away, settling back on the bed. "Go ahead and make your calls. I know a lot of people want to celebrate with you."

She took the phone into the other room because she needed a moment to pull herself together. The whole point of their engagement was to bring them closer. Long distance for another year was the exact opposite.

And, not for the first time, she feared her proposal had been a huge mistake.

**16**

―――――

Ian told himself this fellowship opportunity was not the end of their relationship. He'd told himself that when Kate first shared her good news, and he reminded himself over and over the entire next week—his last week—with Kate. He wasn't going to be the boyfriend that held his brilliant girl-friend back. They'd do long distance. It was no different than the way they'd been before the engagement. He'd thought they'd be doing a year long distance from Boston to Chicago anyway. So now they'd do a year long distance from Boston to Geneva. Except, somehow, between the engagement and living together for a month, that long distance didn't feel quite so doable. In fact, it felt final. And not just because Nate, the guy who adored Kate, would be by her side and not Ian.

He felt like he was losing her.

Everything they did felt like the very last time. Bittersweet. Even stupid little things like looking in the mirror through lipsticked equations got him choked up. Kate must've thought so too because she wasn't as happy as a person who'd just been handed the opportunity of a lifetime should be. She was listless, taking lots of long walks, forgetting to brush her hair. Even her equation writing slowed down. She was in some distant space in her head, seeming to withdraw further and further every day.

Now it was Saturday morning and they had to get ready for the engagement party in their honor in Clover Park. He finished shaving, noting the bathroom mirror was clean for once, the equations wiped away, and went to the bedroom, changing into dress pants and a button-down shirt. Kate was putting in some new earrings, pearls, to go with her new floral dress with cheerful yellow roses. His gaze trailed down her bare legs to sneakers.

"Wrong shoes," he told her.

"Huh?" She glanced down. "Oh. Habit." She kicked them off, went to the closet for her only pair of dress shoes at his place, and came back several minutes later barefoot. By then he was completely ready. He watched her go to the hamper in the corner of the bedroom, pick up all his dirty socks on the floor around it, put them in the hamper, and move the hamper inside the closet.

"I don't know why I didn't think of that before," she said. "Now I don't have to see your socks on the floor and you can play your favorite sock basketball game." Her lower lip trembled, and she rushed out of the room.

He fetched her black heels from the closet and found her in the kitchen, taking eggs and milk out of the refrigerator. "I never cooked for you," she said. "I can make scrambled eggs. I should've cooked for you."

She started opening and shutting cabinets, probably looking for a pan. He set the shoes down and pulled her into his arms. "No time for that," he said. "We need to drive down for the party."

She looked up at him, her eyes shiny with unshed tears. "I need more time," she said urgently. "Today is the party. Then we only have Sunday. I leave Monday morning. We need to cram a lot in." She pulled away. "This is it! I'm not going to see you after this for a year!"

"I'll see you the day before you fly to Europe," he reminded her. "And I'll drive you to the airport." In late August, three months from now, she'd be flying out of New York to go direct to Geneva. She'd be staying at Barry and

Amber's house the day before for a last visit. Their place was about an hour and a half from the airport.

She wrung her hands together. "It's not enough! This month went too fast."

He agreed. Absolutely. But he wasn't going to be the guy holding her back.

He put the eggs and milk away. "You'll be home for Christmas. We'll have a week then." He hadn't accrued enough vacation time at his new job to visit before then.

He turned to find her in the living room, frantically grabbing all the Post-its she'd left on the coffee table. She was already leaving his place.

She crumpled them in her fist and held them up. "These are useless!"

She kept going, rapidly clearing the apartment of all the equations she'd written this past week. She rushed past him, her hands full of crumpled Post-its. "Garbage work!" she exclaimed before shoving them all in the trash can under the kitchen sink.

He took a deep breath, looked around the place, clean and uncluttered for the first time in a month. She'd slowly been cleaning up her stuff all week. Erasing herself from his life. It sucked.

She wiped the equations off the whiteboard on the refrigerator with her hand, leaving black smudges on the side of her hand.

"Kate, your shoes are right there." He pointed to where he'd left the black heels next to her chair at the small kitchen table.

She shoved her feet into the heels and wiped the corners of her eyes, leaving a black smudge on one cheek. "Okay, I'm ready."

Bittersweet.

He crossed to her and took her hand, leading her back to the bathroom. "You want your hair down for the party?"

She sniffled. "I forgot to do my hair. I'm such a mess. I don't even know if I should go to this party."

"We have to go. It's for us."

He set her in front of the sink to take a look at herself. "Oh!" she exclaimed. "Look at my cheek." She ran the water, got some soap, and washed the black smudges off her cheek and hand.

She stared at herself in the mirror, her breathing seeming a little labored. "Why is this so hard?"

He grabbed her hairbrush off the counter and started brushing out her long hair. He didn't need to, it wasn't tangled, he just wanted to. "I guess because now we know how good it is when we're really together, sharing the same space, sharing meals, sharing everything. We'll get there again."

She blinked rapidly. "I don't want to cry. I'm an ugly crier, and my cheeks will be blotchy and my eyes all red and puffy at the party."

He set down the brush, swept her hair to the side, and sank his teeth into the cord of her neck, wanting to short-circuit all the sad thoughts. She jolted. He sucked gently, and she sighed. "Ian."

He turned her in his arms, feeling way too mushy for what he really needed to do, which was pull them both together and get them on the road. So he gripped her hair and kissed her hard and wet and deep until she moaned and clutched his shirt. He broke the kiss and growled in her ear, "Let's go before I fuck you so hard you can't walk straight and then you have to explain that to everyone at the party."

She laughed, and he forced a smile back. He'd hoped to make her laugh, distract her at the very least, but her smile quickly dropped. She bit her lip, her eyes watery behind her glasses. "You're so good to me," she whispered.

His throat was tight, his chest aching. This was going to be hard. This separation. One of them had to keep it together or they'd never get through this party. He turned her toward the door and lightly smacked her ass. "Move it."

She did.

"And leave your hair down," he ordered both because he liked it that way and because he knew she relaxed when he went a little alpha. She always had extra hair bands in her purse.

She tossed her hair over her shoulder and sailed out the front door. He stopped, grabbed the purse she forgot off the foyer table, and followed her out.

~

By the time they showed up at their engagement party, Kate thought they were probably the least happy couple in the place. Ian opened the door to the Jorge Chavez Dance Studio; they stepped inside and were greeted by a chorus of "congratulations!" and people blowing party horns.

Kate grabbed Ian's hand, overwhelmed by the good cheer, especially when she felt so far from celebratory. "Please say something appropriate on behalf of both of us."

He lifted her hand with his. "Thanks, everyone!"

She looked around at the crowd. Amber and Barry had tracked down some of Ian's friends from college and from his old work, along with her parents, his mom, some aunts, uncles, and cousins on both sides, a DJ, a caterer, and a ballroom dance instructor in a black suit, no tie, with what must've been his partner, an elderly woman wearing a skintight orange dress with sequins. It was too far a trip for Kate's Chicago friends to attend. Ian's brother Daniel couldn't make it either but promised to be at the wedding. Who knew when a wedding would happen?

Amber rushed over to hug Kate. "Do you like the decorations?"

Kate blinked and looked around. She hadn't noticed. It was beautiful. Three walls were draped with black velvet with tiny white stars. Strings of white lights ran along the perimeter of the room and in gentle arcs across the ceiling. The center of the room featured a shiny hardwood dance floor.

"I love it," Kate said sincerely.

Amber beamed. "So the plan is, we all get a lesson in the waltz, then food, a champagne toast, and everyone can just dance and have fun after that. Oh! And don't leave without taking your gifts." She pointed over to a table with a large glass bowl full of envelopes.

Kate swallowed over the lump in her throat. Everyone was so happy for them, so generous, yet it felt like Ian was slowly being torn away from her. How was she going to get through this party without crying? She looked around for him and found him talking to his mom. Her parents approached Susan and Ian, and Ian gestured for her to join them.

"Thank you so much for all of this," she told her sister in a strained voice.

"Are you okay, sweetie?" Amber asked.

Kate bit her quivering lower lip. "It's just pretty emotional," she whispered.

Amber nodded sagely. "Completely understand. You can cry if you want. I'll help you fix your makeup after."

"You know I'm an ugly crier."

"And yet Ian would love you even with a bag over your head," Amber said. She lifted a lock of Kate's hair. "Love your hair down. I didn't realize how long it is. So gorgeous, you!"

Kate couldn't smile. "Thank you." Ian communicated with a hard stare that he wanted Kate to join him. It was almost telepathic—*hurry up, I'm dealing with your parents here.* She could read him a lot better now that they'd lived together for a month. "See you," she told Amber.

She hurried as fast as she could over to her parents in her heels. The shoes were only an inch high, but she hadn't worn heels in a very long time. "Hi," she said. "Thank you for coming."

"Of course we would come," her mom said. "I was an integral participant in planning the party logistics."

"Yes, well, thank you for that too," Kate said. Ian's arm slipped around her shoulders.

"Congratulations," her dad said. "When's the wedding?"

"We don't know yet," Kate said. "I'll be away for a year and...it's kinda hard to..." She sucked in air; the room suddenly felt hot and entirely too crowded.

"Most likely when Kate gets back," Ian finished for her.

"Just have to work out the logistics of jobs, living space, all that good stuff; then we'll be set."

"Yes, quite right," her dad said.

"You changed your earrings!" her mom exclaimed. "Shanna told us to wait four weeks. It's only been two weeks."

Kate pushed her hair back to better show off her new pearl earrings. "I don't follow the rules. I'm a badass rebel."

Ian threw back his head and laughed. She couldn't help laughing along with him. The whole badass rebel thing was new for her.

Her mom's brows drew together. "I hope you're still focused on your work. You're destined for great things. I read your last publication—"

"I don't want to talk about work right now," Kate said. "I just want to enjoy my party." Not really. But her mom could go on and on about the importance of discipline and focus in the sciences, and Kate was just not in the mood.

Barry came over then, congratulating them both and handing Violet over to Kate's mom. "Grandmom time," Barry announced.

Violet hugged her grandmom and then poked her star earrings. Grandmom even cracked a smile.

"Amber needs my help with something," Barry said. He winked at Kate and took off.

She wondered what Barry was up to, but then Ian grabbed her hand. "Come on, badass rebel, let's go make the rounds."

After they said hi and accepted congratulations from a lot of people, the DJ got on the mike and announced the bride and groom should report to the dance floor. Although technically they weren't yet bride and groom, Kate took that as her cue. Of course, it was hard not to with Ian already pulling her along. They stopped in the center where the instructor and his partner were waiting.

"Hello, I'm Jorge, your instructor for the evening, and this beautiful woman is my wife and forever dance partner, Maggie."

Ian shook Jorge's hand. "Ian, the groom. And this is Kate."

Jorge took Kate's hand. "So nice to meet you," he said, and then kissed the back of her hand. Whoa. He was very handsome for a middle-aged man. His black hair was slicked back, his golden tanned skin glowed, and he had a fit dancer's body.

"You too," Kate said. She giggled, and Ian's head swiveled to her. She shrugged.

Maggie curtsied. She looked older than her husband, but spry, her white hair stuck up in little spikes, her blue eyes were bright and sharp. "Congratulations, you two!"

"Thank you," Kate and Ian said practically in unison.

Maggie eyed Ian. "You a showboat like your brother? We've seen him bust a move on many occasions."

Ian smiled and shook his head. "Nope. Barry's the performer. I only know the eighth-grade shuffle."

"Ah, well. You are in for a treat!" Maggie exclaimed. "Tell him, foxy!" she said to her foxy husband.

Jorge inclined his head. "It's a box step. I'll demonstrate with Maggie, and then you'll try. Once you feel comfortable, we'll do it with music."

Kate and Ian watched as Jorge took Maggie's hand and rested his other hand on her back just below her shoulder blade. "And one, two, three," he said, moving them in a box step. Kate was pleased to see it really was a box. Forward, side, side, backward, side, side, a perfect geometric square. This would be easy.

After they danced for a short time, Jorge stopped and turned to her and Ian. "Now, you."

She stood in front of Ian. He took her hand and pressed his other hand to her back. Jorge moved her hand from Ian's arm to his shoulder. "Good," Jorge said. "Now, Ian, you lead, your hand on her back guides her, the hand holding hers is the lightest touch."

"Sometimes the hips take the lead too!" Maggie chortled.

"This is true," Jorge said with a hot look for his wife. He turned back to them. "Give it a try."

Kate had never had a dance lesson, never done a sport, so it was understandable that she stepped on Ian's feet a lot and tripped once. After the fourth toe crunch, Ian pulled away, wincing. Kate's cheeks burned, and she glanced over to Jorge for his reaction. Maggie had already left to talk to the caterer, the red-headed chef Shane O'Hare. Everyone knew Shane from his ice cream shop in town. She kinda wished she could join them.

Jorge rushed over, a patient smile on his face. "This is no problem. May I suggest you remove your heels? They seem to be affecting your footwork."

"Yes," Kate said with some relief. Her heels were killing her after an hour of being on her feet. She crossed the dance floor and set them out of the way. When she returned, Jorge was in deep conversation with Ian. They got quiet once she got to them. "Everything okay?"

"It's all good," Ian said, pulling her flush against him, his hand on her back. They were pelvis to pelvis, and she flushed with heat. He took her other hand for the waltz position. "We're going to try once more," Ian said, "and then we'll do it to music while Jorge invites everyone to join us."

"Oh, that would be good," she whispered. "I feel like everyone's watching us."

He glanced around. "Some are, some aren't. Ready?"

"Sure."

"And one, two, three," Jorge counted for them.

And this time they really waltzed. Or Ian did, anyway. There was no way for her to mess up because his entire body pressed along hers and he practically lifted her with him. He took her all around the dance floor, making them look graceful and gloriously romantic. Her prince.

When they finished, everyone applauded.

Ian grinned at her. "Smooth moves, Kate."

"That was all you and you know it," she whispered.

He dipped her suddenly over his arm and slowly pulled her back up.

"Ian," she breathed, her gaze locked on his. The air sizzled between them.

Maggie clapped, breaking the spell. "Everyone join the happy couple."

The music started, and everyone danced with them in their own version of waltz. Barry danced her sister around beautifully like they'd done this many times before. Susan claimed Violet for a dance, and Kate witnessed her parents dancing for the first time ever. Her parents talked the entire time, probably about work, but they seemed happy. Maggie and Jorge managed to get everyone on the dance floor and then joined in

She gazed into Ian's warm loving brown eyes and tried to memorize every detail about the moment. His strong arms, his large hand splayed on her back possessively, his scent woodsy with a hint of citrus, the small crooked smile that said he loved her and would do dirty things to her later.

It was the best time.

A mushy heart-squeezing celebration.

The last best memory to get her through the dark times ahead.

**17**

———

Ian was damn tired of saying goodbye to Kate. When he'd first suggested they try a long-distance relationship, he hadn't counted on how close they would get during their brief times together, making each goodbye that much more painful. He'd dropped her off at the airport the Monday after their engagement party and Kate had cried. Not like a few tears leaking out either. Big sobbing tears like he'd never seen from her. It killed him. Nothing he said soothed her. No amount of promising to stay in touch or reminders that he'd see her at the end of August made a difference.

She drifted further away from him once she got back to Chicago. Over the next three months, Kate threw herself into her work, needing to do as much as possible in preparation for her time in Geneva. She didn't want to do phone sex and had informed him she went off the pill, not because she planned on sleeping with other people, because she planned on being celibate for the next year. A true scholar focused only on work.

It was like she'd already said goodbye to him.

He couldn't visit her in Chicago due to a lack of vacation time, but he damn sure was going to see her at his brother's house before she flew out to Geneva. The day finally arrived. A Saturday, the last weekend in August, and her flight was early Sunday morning. He pulled into the driveway of Barry and Amber's house, grabbed the bouquet of red roses from the passenger seat, and headed to the door.

He knocked, and Barry answered. "Those for me?" his brother asked. "How sweet!"

"Ha-ha," Ian said, pushing past him. "Where's Kate? Kate!" he called.

She appeared from the kitchen with Violet on her hip. His heart lodged in his throat. For a weird hallucinatory moment, he felt like he'd come home to his wife with his daughter on her hip.

"Hi," Kate said softly.

"Fwowerth!" Violet exclaimed, bouncing a little and pointing at the bouquet.

He closed the distance between them. "I missed you so much."

Kate blinked rapidly. "I missed you too. Are those for me?"

"Yes."

She set Violet down, and he wrapped Kate in his arms, at long last. She rested her head on his chest and let out a sigh.

One day. That was all they had before another goodbye.

He pulled back and handed her the roses. She buried her nose in them. "Thank you. I guess I'll have to leave them here tomorrow, but—"

"You can enjoy them today," Amber said, coming downstairs. "Hi, Ian."

"Hey," he said.

Amber went to his side and hugged him. "I'll put these in a vase for you," she said, taking the bouquet.

"Congratulations," Ian said, belatedly remembering Amber was newly pregnant.

Amber beamed. "Thank you."

"She's due in March," Kate said. "The new baby might even share a birthday with Violet."

Violet clung to her mom's leg, looking worried. "And congratulations to you too," he told Violet. "You're going to be a big sister, which is awesome. I'm sure you'll get a big sister present from the baby." He'd send one anyway.

Violet's brown eyes widened. "The baby get present? Yay!"

"We'll see," Barry said.

Ian made a small gesture to his brother to let him know he'd be sending one.

"Definitely," Amber said. "How exciting to be a big sister! I am too, to Aunt Kate."

"Best big sister there is," Kate said.

Violet looked from Kate to her mom and beamed. She let go of Amber's leg and went to play with her dollhouse.

They spent the day playing with Violet, hanging out with Barry and Amber, and talking about Kate's setup in Geneva. She had a studio apartment in a building where a lot of single scientists roomed. He guessed that Nate would also be rooming in the building, but didn't bring it up. He didn't want to think about it. Kate hadn't said boo about the fact that he worked with his ex, Morgan, even more now that funding had increased on her project. And so he would do the same. Even if he hated it. Anyway, she didn't have to worry about Morgan, who was apparently sleeping with Shawn, the engineer that shared a workspace with her project. Ian could care less as long as they both got their work done.

Kate told them more about the particle accelerator where she'd be running her experiments, which was larger than he'd realized, a twenty-seven-mile ring of superconducting magnets underground between Switzerland and France. The particles moved at the speed of light. No wonder Kate wanted to run experiments there. Nothing like it was available stateside.

They had a quiet dinner at home, and then finally he and Kate went to bed a little early to spend time together before her early flight.

He pulled her close in the dark of the bedroom, both of them naked under the covers, and just held her. He'd so missed her curvy little body. And not just for sex. He'd gotten used to her curling up against his side during their month of living together. He'd had to buy a body pillow and put it in her place to get any sleep after she went back to Chicago.

"It's different now, isn't it?" she whispered. "I mean, between us."

"Because we got in deep."

"Maybe too deep," she said softly. "It hurts to see you."

Unfortunately, he knew what she meant. It wasn't that he didn't want to see her, but it did hurt because then she'd be ripped away from him again, taking another piece of his heart with her. Too many more goodbyes and he'd be walking around with a hollow chest.

He slid his hand into her hair, cupping her soft cheek, and kissed her. He pulled back when he felt a tear touch his cheek. "Don't cry," he said, brushing the tears from her cheeks. "Please. Let's just forget about tomorrow and enjoy right now."

"I can't help it," she said in a quivery voice. At least it wasn't those big gulping sobs that were like a stabbing knife to his heart.

He rolled on top of her, settling between her legs. "Let me help you forget," he said, speaking close to her ear and then skimming kisses along the side of her neck. She let out a shuddery breath and ran her fingers through the hair at the nape of his neck.

"Yes," she said on a sigh.

He went slow, kissing and stroking and tasting, memorizing every part of her, every sigh, every shudder. His heart thudded against his chest because this was truly making love, every touch meant to convey just how much he loved her.

When they finally joined, their fingers entwined, gazes locked on each other, he kissed her tenderly. "I love you, Kate. You take that with you. Hold it close in your heart."

"I love you too," she said, her voice wobbly. "You are my heart."

He dropped his forehead to hers, overwhelmed with emotion. They shared a breath and then another. He wanted to merge with her, to never separate again.

She wiggled under him. "Make it good. Gimme a ten."

He laughed and gave her a hard kiss. "You know I set that bar."

She dug her heels into his ass. "Show me what you got."

He did. And she let go; he felt the moment she did, bucking wildly under him, heard the moment she did as she urged him on, "Faster, harder, ohgod, ohgod, ohgod." He covered her mouth with his, swallowing her cries of ecstasy as she climaxed and took him with her. She trembled under him in the aftermath of joined pleasure and all-consuming love. He rolled to his side, pulling her close and holding her tight.

He woke her in the middle of the night, joining with her again in another slow tender loving, both of them caught in a timeless space, lost in the moment.

All too soon, it was morning.

She packed up quickly. They said their goodbyes to Barry, Amber, and Violet, and got on the road.

Kate was quiet. He really hoped she didn't cry when he dropped her off at the airport. He couldn't promise to hold it together for another airport goodbye. They'd both be a mess.

"You okay?" he finally asked after a long fifteen-minute silence where he had entirely too much time to think about their goodbye.

"No," she said softly.

"I'll see you at Christmas," he said.

A beat passed in silence. He glanced over at her. She took off her glasses and cleaned them with the end of her shirt. He tensed, knowing her tells, knowing something bad was coming.

She slid her glasses back on, wrung her hands together in her lap, and stared at them. "Our timing has never been right," she said quietly.

"We'll get there," he said, though he knew she was right. The first time they'd gotten together, she'd been too young. The second time they got together was just before she left for Chicago. And now they were together and about to have an ocean between them.

She went on. "We should've waited until we were both in

a stable place in our lives so we wouldn't have to go through all this back and forth."

"I don't regret a moment I've had with you," he said fiercely.

She let out a hiccupping sob. The heart-wrenching kind that killed him.

"Kate…" He didn't know what to say. There was no way of making it easier for either of them.

"I never should've proposed," she said on a sob. "I'm sorry."

He glanced over at her red eyes, red nose, tears pouring down her cheeks. "Please, Kate, don't—"

"I caught you unawares with my sur—" her breath caught on a sob "—*stupid* surprise. I dragged you into an engagement when I should've waited for the right time and the right place." She sniffled and wiped her nose with the back of her hand.

His stomach clenched. "Don't do this." He could feel it. She was cutting ties.

"I'm not breaking up with you. I'm just ending the engagement. It was too much, too soon."

"I'm okay with it," he said. "I know I had cold feet at first, but I'm good now."

She sucked in a shuddering breath. "I think we need to step back a little."

"I refuse. I'm still engaged."

"It's easier this way. Okay? We don't have rings. We haven't set a date. We'll return to it when the timing is right."

"No."

She got quiet, wiping her tears and staring out the window.

And even though he'd refused to go along with ending the engagement, he felt like it was over. They drove in heavy silence the rest of the way there. He parked at short-term parking so he could walk her to the terminal.

She stopped him, grabbing him by the sleeve before he could exit the car. "No. We'll say goodbye here. I don't want to cry in the airport."

He pulled her close and hugged her.

She pulled away much too soon. "I'll be in touch." But she didn't say when. She didn't have a schedule. His Kate loved schedules.

He pushed a lock of hair back from her face. "I'll call Friday night for phone sex, Sunday night for talk." That was their old schedule, which had narrowed to Sunday night talk over the last few months.

He was losing her.

She shook her head. "There's a six-hour time difference. I don't know what I'll be doing when."

"We'll see, okay?" He was scrambling for purchase on the edge of a cliff. "We'll play it by ear."

She nodded. "Sure, okay." She grabbed her purse off the floor of the car. "I'll just get my suitcase. Pop the trunk." She stepped out of the car.

He pressed the button to pop the trunk, got out, and met her by the trunk. He watched her get her small wheeled suitcase and laptop bag out, looking cool and distant, all tucked tight behind her serious scientist exterior.

This was a woman saying goodbye. Maybe for good.

She held the handle of her wheeled suitcase in one hand, laptop bag on top, and slid her purse strap higher on her shoulder. She gave him a curt nod. "Goodbye."

"I love you, Kate."

Her lower lip wobbled, and she bit it. She met his eyes briefly. "I love you too."

"Call me when you get there."

"It'll be late. I won't be able to use my phone. I need to pick up an international cell phone." She looked off toward the terminal and back to him. "I'll text you when I can."

And with that she turned and strode toward her new life. Without him.

## 18

____________

Kate quickly settled into a satisfying routine in Geneva. The new environment invigorated her, surrounded by fellow physicists, deep in conversations with Nate and new colleagues from around the world. Nate lived just down the hall from her. He brought her quality coffee every morning, and they commuted to work together in the car he'd bought upon arrival. If she'd never met Ian, never known what true love really was, she might've ended up with someone like Nate. He was a true work partner, the kind her mom had highly recommended, yet once they completed their work, she found she just wanted to be alone. He invited her out for cocktails with their peers, regularly invited her to sightseeing excursions, but all she wanted to do was take long walks. Didn't matter where. Snow, rain, sun didn't matter either. Just walk and walk and walk. Alone with her thoughts on her work, complete and total focus. After only four months, she was getting great data, very near to proving her theory.

Yet she felt empty.

She kept in touch with Ian, as promised. They talked on the phone, texted, and emailed, but it wasn't the same. She couldn't shake the melancholy, and she couldn't even smile at his jokes. At Thanksgiving, after she'd had an odd meal of chicken instead of turkey with the other ex-pat Americans, which made her more sad and homesick than ever, she called Ian. It was still afternoon back in Clover Park, and she could hear their family in the background at Barry and Amber's house. She held the phone slightly away from her mouth so she could hear him, and he wouldn't hear her quiet sobs. He knew her well, though, and got right to the point.

"It's not working, is it?" Ian asked. "This long-distance thing. It's making you miserable."

She sniffled. "I'm sorry."

"Don't be sorry. I was the one who pushed for a long-distance relationship."

A beat passed in silence. She *was* miserable. But she didn't want to say goodbye.

"I'm holding you back," he said.

"You're not," she protested. "As miserable as I am, I'm seeing great results with my research."

"I want you to be happy, Kate," he said gently.

She forced the words past the lump in her throat. "I'll see you in four weeks. Only four more weeks."

"You sure?"

"Yes."

"Okay. I'll pick you up at the airport." She heard Barry calling for Ian in the background.

"Time to eat?" she asked.

"Yeah, everyone's going to the table."

"Have some well-cooked turkey for me," she said, trying for a joke about the badly cooked turkey she'd made him once.

"I will. Love you." He was distracted, surrounded by his loving family, not needing her.

"Love you too. Bye."

She hung up, hugged her middle tightly, and then cried her eyes out.

When Kate landed in New York just before Christmas, she headed briskly through the airport to where Ian had told her to meet him outside of baggage claim. She gave herself a pep talk that had been her mantra the whole flight over (until she conked out). *You will enjoy each moment. You will not think of goodbye.*

It was afternoon in New York. They had ten days. She'd be flying back on New Year's Day and not seeing him again until March, when he would finally have the vacation time to visit. Another goodbye after that.

*You will enjoy each moment. You will not think of goodbye.*

She stepped outside to a crisp cold day and quickly scanned the line of cars and taxis waiting. She spotted Ian within seconds, standing next to his car, holding up a neon pink poster board that read Kate Lewis-Furnukle. There were even blue glitter stars around it that she suspected her sister had something to do with. Her stomach churned. Even though she knew he was trying to be sweet, the hyphenated name just reminded her of their engagement that ended with an ocean between them. All of it was her stupid fault. Her stupid idea.

She rushed over to him, her suitcase bumping along behind her, and stopped short next to him. "Ian, I thought we agreed no engagement until things are more settled between us."

"Hello to you too," he said and bopped her on the head with the poster. He grinned. "You have glitter in your hair."

She was about to accuse him of putting it there when he kissed her. She lost her train of thought as her body remembered everything that was right about their joining. She sank against him.

"Get in the car," he said, taking her suitcase and slipping her laptop bag from her shoulder. He headed for the trunk.

She shook out her hair, trying to get the glitter out. Then she got in the car, pulled down the visor mirror, and saw blue glitter on her cheeks. She got a tissue from her purse and wiped it away.

Ian got in and pulled away from the curb. "Did you sleep on the plane?"

"Yes, though I fear my sleep schedule is going to be completely screwed up."

"Well, I'm glad you slept because I want you awake for this next part."

"What next part?"

"You'll see," he said with his adorable crooked smile. "I have a surprise for you."

"Really?"

He gave her a warm look. "Yeah, really."

She leaned back in her seat, her brain cranking, trying to guess what he had in mind. They were supposed to be going to Ian's apartment in Boston for a couple of days and then driving down to Clover Park to spend Christmas Day with Barry, Amber, and Violet.

"Is the surprise at your apartment?" she asked. She'd really been looking forward to going back to his apartment to make love. She hadn't had sex or even pulled out her vibrator (named Ian for obvious reasons) in *four* long months. Her libido had fled when the melancholy set in.

"You'll see," he answered mysteriously.

"I hope we'll get to your private apartment soon," she said. *Hint, hint.*

"Maybe we will, maybe we won't."

It seemed Ian was in no hurry to make love. She stared out the window, puzzling over this newest surprise.

After a while, she realized they weren't heading to Boston. In fact, Ian appeared to be heading into Manhattan. He'd completely missed the turnoff for 95 N. This meant a delay in their lovemaking. How could he not want to go straight to bed after *four* long celibate months?

"Have you been orgasming without me?" she asked.

He glanced over, a small smile playing over his lips. "Now why would you ask that?"

"Because we're heading into Manhattan. Did you know I haven't had a single orgasm since the last one we had together in August?"

"Why didn't you use Ian?" he asked, referring to her vibrator.

"I wasn't in the mood."

He chuckled.

"It's not funny. I've been waiting all this time, and now you're making me wait longer. Why are we going to the city?"

"It's part of the surprise, my little monkey."

She huffed. He'd definitely been orgasming without her. Not that she thought he was with someone else. He still ended each phone call with an *I love you*, but clearly his libido had not been strained one bit by their separation.

Soon Central Park came into view. She sat up a little straighter in her seat. The horse-drawn carriages were decorated with greenery and cheerful bells for the holidays. Ian kept going, and she took in white lights around the small trees lining the sidewalks, stores with beautiful window displays, and a Santa on the corner, ringing a bell.

Ian pulled into a parking garage. "Come on."

She got out and joined him. He passed the key to a valet, and they walked outside.

"Are we Christmas shopping?" she asked. She wouldn't mind. She still had to get a gift for Violet. She had some small handmade ornaments from Geneva for Barry and Amber. Ian's gift was going to be some lingerie she hoped to pick up in Boston.

"Nope."

"Are you going to give me a hint?"

"Nope."

And that was all he said. He took her hand, and they walked at a leisurely pace. She peeked into the store windows at the moving displays of dolls and tiny electric trains through tiny villages.

"I always wanted a tiny Christmas village like that one," she said, pointing to the display.

He stopped short. "Please tell me your parents let you have a Christmas tree."

"We did."

"Good. I'll let them live."

She smiled to herself. It was nice the way Ian looked out for her. They kept going all the way to Central Park. She stopped near the line of horse-drawn carriages. "I always wanted to do one of those carriage rides," she said wistfully.

"Then it's your lucky day," he said with a grin. "Come on."

He led her to a beautiful white carriage that said *reserved* on the bench seat. Ian spoke to the driver, who nodded and took the reserved sign off.

"Ian! Is this the surprise? I love it!"

"Good." He held out his hand to help her in. "My lady."

She climbed up, feeling giddy. The driver turned in his seat. "Happy holidays, miss."

"You too!" she exclaimed. This was so romantic! She'd always wanted to do a horse-drawn carriage ride. Ian sat next to her and took a small folded blanket from the side and covered both of their laps.

The driver signaled to the beautiful white horse, and they trotted off, the bells jingling in time to the clip-clop of the horse's feet. She looked all around the park and the city as they made their way around the perimeter of the park.

"Kate!"

She turned to find Ian holding a small black velvet box. "I said—"

"Ian! What are you doing?"

"I said I never got you a ring. And I should have because this engagement was always very real to me." He opened the box to a platinum band with a round solitaire diamond.

"You didn't need to get me a ring," she whispered, but she couldn't take her eyes off it. She'd never worn a ring before. It was exquisite.

"Marry me, Kate."

Her eyes snapped to his. "But I thought we agreed it was too hard to be engaged long distance."

"Can you please just wear the ring?" he asked in an unusually patient voice.

She smiled and nodded. He slid it on her finger and it fit perfectly.

She stared at it. "I've never worn a ring before. How did you know my size?"

"Amber helped me. You're similar sizes."

She met his warm brown eyes, the enormity of the

moment suddenly sinking in. "Ian," she managed over the lump in her throat, "this was a very nice surprise."

He kissed her tenderly. "There's more."

"Really?" She couldn't imagine what else he could possibly have planned that was better than a romantic horse-drawn carriage ride and a diamond engagement ring with a besotted fiancé proposal.

He stroked her cheek. "Really. New Year's Eve wedding."

"What!" she screeched so loudly the horse whinnied. "There's no time to plan that! And we both said no long-distance marriage."

He took both her hands in his. "I planned it with Hailey and Amber. I got the license. I just need the bride."

"But long distance—"

"We're done with that."

"What!" she screeched.

He grinned. "That's the last surprise. I couldn't wait another five months to be with you. Couldn't bear another goodbye. But five months is pretty short to keep a valuable employee happy."

Her breath caught. Could it be? Could he really be joining her in Geneva?

"What do you mean?" she demanded. "Spell it out."

He flashed a smile. "My boss is letting me work remotely for five months as long as I fly back once a month for a few days to check in."

"Can you afford all that travel?"

"I've got frequent flier miles from traveling so much from my old job. And now that my boss is on board...we're a go."

She slapped a hand over her mouth. "Omigod, I can't believe it!"

She threw her arms around him, crying happy tears this time. He held her for a long time. Finally, she lifted her head and looked up at him. "Did I make a mistake proposing to you too soon?"

He tapped the end of her nose. "It was early, wasn't it? After only three months of dating."

She deflated. "I guess."

He smiled warmly. "But if you hadn't proposed, we wouldn't have had a chance to see how good we were together before you went away. So I'd say if it was a mistake, it was a good mistake."

She shook her head. "I can't believe it! I thought I was going to be so sad when I had to say goodbye and miss you so much, but it's really happening. This is our happy ever after!"

"I never doubted for a moment."

"Really?"

He kissed her. "Well, maybe for a tiny chimp-size moment."

"I love you so much," she said.

"I love you too," he said against her mouth, and then they were kissing.

And she didn't have to think of goodbye. She thought of nothing, her brain blissfully quiet, lost in the moment.

**EPILOGUE**

Kate had her fairy-tale wedding. She was truly Cinderella for the day from her tiara to her poufy white gown to her silver slippers decorated with crystals. They married at Ludbury House, the same mansion where her sister married, and it was glorious. Ian even wore a top hat and tails and had arranged for a horse-drawn carriage to carry them off afterward through Main Street in Clover Park back to Barry and Amber's house, where they spent their honeymoon night before flying back to Geneva together on New Year's Day.

The five months in Geneva flew by with Ian at her side. They were squashed together in a studio apartment, which made for frequent territorial flare-ups (from both of them) and frequent makeup sex. A thoroughly enjoyable experience. They had fun sightseeing on weekends and even made it over to Paris for a week for a romantic honeymoon.

Now it was July, she was happy to be Dr. Lewis-Furrukle (such a mouthful, ha-ha) and had begun her new assistant professor job at her alma mater MIT. She hadn't gotten a Nobel Prize for her work; she wasn't even in the running because her research had proven inconclusive. Nonetheless, she'd published her results that opened up some new fields of inquiry. That was enough for her to field multiple job offers.

MIT came out on top, not just because Ian worked there, but because her former physics professor knew her work well and offered her a very sweet deal. They would be funding her research and sponsoring her to travel on a short-term basis to whatever facility she needed anywhere in the world. She couldn't have predicted a more perfect fit between her career and her personal life.

They lived in Ian's apartment and were still scouting the area for a house, made possible in large part from her parents' generous wedding gift. She hoped their future children were of an analytical bent because they could save considerably on college tuition if the children attended MIT. It was an alternative scenario in her financial spreadsheet. Ian left all that planning up to her. He liked to go with the flow, and she made sure the flow went in the right direction. They were happy, gloriously so. And because she loved how well her first surprise for him had worked out, she had another surprise to pop on him in about six months.

Of course, she was too excited to wait that long. So she'd been giving him subtle hints, waiting for him to notice her small but gratifying baby bump. He'd been shockingly obtuse. She kept turning sideways next to him, yet he hadn't said a word about her newly pooching stomach. Considerate beast. She'd have to be more obvious. For crying out loud, she was twelve weeks already!

Tonight she stood sideways next to their bed, completely naked. She really couldn't have been more obvious than that. Ian was already in bed. She launched into a detailed description of her day.

"Get over here," Ian growled.

He reached for her, and she dodged out of his grasp.

She resumed her sideways stance. His boxer briefs flew right past her head where they landed near the hamper just inside the open closet. He was a terrible basketball laundry player, but she never complained because laundry was his job, and he did it well.

"Have you made any progress on the companion robot?"

she asked politely, jutting out her hip to make her belly more pronounced.

His voice dropped to a low scraping register that made her pulse thrum. "Don't make me come get you."

She tossed her hair over her shoulder and pushed her stomach out even more. "Notice anything different?"

"Did you get a haircut?"

She stood up straight and slammed her hands on her hips. "No," she huffed.

Geez! She couldn't believe Ian hadn't noticed this huge baby bump. Okay, not huge. But it was something! She glanced down to be sure. Her stomach was not flat like it used to be.

She met his eyes to find him smiling rather deviously. "Why are you smiling?"

"Because I'm about to do dirty things to you."

She held up a hand and resumed her sideways pose. "You're ruining the surprise. If you don't catch on soon, I'm going to have to tell you, and where's the surprise in that?" She ran her hand over her belly in the most obvious of gestures. Sometimes the male needed a direct clue.

"Hmm…" he drawled and rubbed his chin like he was thinking really hard.

"Yes?"

He shook his head. "Oh, no. I know better than to say anything about that growing belly. That's just my good cooking. A compliment to the chef."

She narrowed her eyes and made one last-ditch obvious effort. "Something is cooking, and it's all your doing."

He leaned back on his elbows, giving her a thorough once-over. "Sorry. I don't do subtle. Spell it out."

She put her hands on her hips and faced him. "You do so do subtle! I'm the one who doesn't do subtle!"

He sat up and reached for her again. She darted out of reach and resumed her sideways hip-jutting, huge-belly-protruding pose. She lifted her chin and looked off in the distance so her expression wouldn't give it away.

"Are you practicing to be a model?" he asked.

She bit back a laugh. "Yes, I'm practicing to be a nude model."

"I knew it." She could hear the smile in his voice.

She turned to him, met his warm brown eyes, and melted. "You know."

He grinned. "Congratulations to me. And you. Now get over here, you tempting seductress."

She crawled over the mattress to him, and he grabbed her and rolled her under him. He stroked her cheek, gazing at her tenderly, then stroked down her throat, leaving a tingling trail.

"How long have you known?" she whispered.

He kissed her. "Since I planted my seed, little monkey."

"You did not know then! I didn't know then."

He gave her his crooked adorable smile.

"For real, when did you know?" she asked.

He started kissing his way down her body. Her limbs got heavy, and her eyes fluttered closed. Short-circuited and loving it.

He spoke again when he reached her belly and kissed it reverently. "I knew when you started decorating the apartment with curtains and throw blankets and framed pictures of our family. I knew when your equations turned into hearts and stars. I knew when you started polling random women with strollers for the pain level of labor on a scale of one to ten. I knew—"

"Okay! So I'm not so great at surprises."

He dropped a kiss on her sex, making her jolt, before levering back up to kiss her on the mouth. "I'm just great at you."

"Am I great at you?"

He kissed the corner of her mouth, then the other corner, and when her lips parted on a sigh, he claimed her mouth. The kiss went on and on, and then something changed and it turned harder, rougher, deeper.

He tore his mouth away. "Let's see how great you are at me. What am I thinking right now?"

"You want a hard screw, but you're worried about the baby, so you're thinking of going down on me instead," she suggested.

He kissed her and bit her lower lip. "Brilliant, she's brilliant. And so subtle too." He was onto her with her subtle suggestions. She didn't care because he obliged, kissing his way down her body until he reached her favorite spot. The spot he owned.

He sucked hard, and she saw stars. He lifted his head, arranging her legs over his shoulders. "Tell me everything you've learned so far about pregnancy and labor in great detail," he said, which got her excited because, boy, did she know a lot.

"The first trimester can be..." Her brain shut down as he lapped at her. "Ohgod, ohgod, ohgod."

"Keep talking," he said and resumed the sweet torture.

"Please. Oh god." She tensed, already so close. He stopped, and she grabbed his head, trying to push him back down. It didn't work.

"Fascinating," he said. "What else, darling? I love hearing you talk."

"Please," she begged. He lowered his head again. She was lost. "Don't stop, don't stop, don't stop," she chanted as she climbed and climbed and climbed.

She lost the power of speech and then she flew. The entire galaxy appeared behind her eyes, and she was soaring among the stars. She was vaguely aware of Ian shifting, and then he lifted her, settling her on top of him. His hands on her hips guided her down on him really, really slow. She realized with a start that he'd been doing this the past several times they made love, and now she knew why. He was being careful of the baby. Her heart filled with mushy overwhelming love.

She leaned down and kissed him. "I love you so much."

"Love you too. Lean back, darling, I'm gonna make you see stars again."

"How did you know I see stars?"

"You talk about it after you come."

She did? She was in such a weird out-of-her-mind place she didn't realize. "What do I say?"

"Stars, just one word, in a reverent grateful tone."

"Grateful!"

And then he was moving her, guiding her to his rhythm. She ran her hand through her hair, relaxed and filled with pleasure.

"So we're twelve weeks," he said, startling her. She hadn't told him how far along she was. She kept track of it on a very informative website with week-by-week ultrasound pictures showing the development of the baby.

She leaned her hands on his shoulders to get a good look at him. "Are you spying on me?"

One corner of his mouth lifted. "You put a square around the date you start your period on the kitchen calendar. I can do math."

"Yes, we're twelve weeks." She liked the way he said "we," though she wished "we" could share the pain of mo-fo labor her sister had told her about in great gory detail recently. Though Amber declared it all worth it when she held her newborn son, Wyatt, in her arms. Kate had to agree. Wyatt was a little over three months and adorable.

Ian's hand slid down her spine, bringing a hot tingle. He cupped her ass. "Notice how I didn't pass out at this baby news."

She grinned, remembering when he'd passed out over her fake baby news back when she'd first proposed to him. She kissed him and sucked his lower lip into her mouth. He thrust, taking her deep and holding her there, joined tightly together.

"You must be ready for a permanent commitment with me," she said, her breath coming a little faster now.

He pressed his hand with the wedding band on it against hers. "I guess so."

"You guess so!" And then she rode him wicked fast and hard, short-circuiting his teasing ways and reminding him he was hers.

Afterwards, she collapsed on top of him, her cheek to his chest, listening to his wildly thumping heart.

Ian finally spoke. "Damn, woman. I didn't think you could get any hornier. This pregnancy thing is really working for me."

She giggled and then sighed in contentment. "Me too."

Don't miss my new standalone series about the irresistibly sexy Campbell brothers (and a tomboy sister) who find love with the help of the matchmaking leader of the Happy Endings Book Club. *Hidden Hollywood* (Happy Endings Book Club #1) is available now.

**She's on top…**

When superstar actress Claire Jordan researched her role for the Fierce Trilogy movies, she never expected the bond she feels with the author and her romance book club aka the Happy Endings Book Club. Soon Claire finds herself confessing her secret longing for a regular guy—no more egocentric wealthy players—and the book club is all too ready to help. In disguise as a regular girl, she's all set for a date with book-club-approved Josh Campbell.

**He's on top…**

Billionaire tech CEO Jake Campbell is weary of gold-digging women, especially the glamorous superficial types. So when his identical twin, Josh, calls in a favor, asking Jake to step in as him on a date, Jake figures one of Josh's cute girl-next-door types might be just what he needs. One night of passion with the sweet girl next door leaves Jake wanting more, except she seems to have vanished.

Sometimes a Happy Ending is just the beginning.

Sign up for my newsletter and never miss a new release! https://www.kyliegilmore.com/newsletter

# ALSO BY KYLIE GILMORE

**Unleashed Romance <<steamy romcoms with dogs!**

Fetching (Book 1)

Dashing (Book 2)

Sporting (Book 3)

Toying (Book 4)

Blazing (Book 5)

Chasing (Book 6)

Daring (Book 7)

Leading (Book 8)

Racing (Book 9)

Loving (Book 10)

**The Clover Park Series <<brothers who put family first!**

The Opposite of Wild (Book 1)

Daisy Does It All (Book 2)

Bad Taste in Men (Book 3)

Kissing Santa (Book 4)

Restless Harmony (Book 5)

Not My Romeo (Book 6)

Rev Me Up (Book 7)

An Ambitious Engagement (Book 8)

Clutch Player (Book 9)

A Tempting Friendship (Book 10)

Clover Park Bride: Nico and Lily's Wedding

A Valentine's Day Gift (Book 11)

Maggie Meets Her Match (Book 12)

**The Clover Park Charmers series <<sweet and sexy charmers!**

Almost Over It (Book 1)

Almost Married (Book 2)

Almost Fate (Book 3)

Almost in Love (Book 4)

Almost Romance (Book 5)

Almost Hitched (Book 6)

**Happy Endings Book Club Series <<the Campbell family and a romance book club collide!**

Hidden Hollywood (Book 1)

Inviting Trouble (Book 2)

So Revealing (Book 3)

Formal Arrangement (Book 4)

Bad Boy Done Wrong (Book 5)

Mess With Me (Book 6)

Resisting Fate (Book 7)

Chance of Romance (Book 8)

Wicked Flirt (Book 9)

An Inconvenient Plan (Book 10)

A Happy Endings Wedding (Book 11)

**The Rourkes Series <<swoonworthy princes and kickass princesses!**

Royal Catch (Book 1)

Royal Hottie (Book 2)

Royal Darling (Book 3)

Royal Charmer (Book 4)

Royal Player (Book 5)

Royal Shark (Book 6)

Rogue Prince (Book 7)

Rogue Gentleman (Book 8)

Rogue Rascal (Book 9)

Rogue Angel (Book 10)

Rogue Devil (Book 11)

Rogue Beast (Book 12)

**Check out my website for the most up-to-date list of my books:
kyliegilmore.com/books**

# ABOUT THE AUTHOR

Kylie Gilmore is the *USA Today* bestselling author of over fifty humorous contemporary romances. Her series include Unleashed Romance, the Rourkes, the Happy Endings Book Club, Clover Park, and Clover Park Charmers. With more than three million downloads of her books, readers all over the world love escaping into her hilarious feel-good romances featuring strong bonds with family, friends, and community.

Kylie lives in New York with her family, a demanding cat, and a nutso dog. When she's not writing, reading hot romance, or dutifully taking notes at writing conferences, you can find her flexing her muscles all the way to the high cabinet for her secret chocolate stash.

Sign up for Kylie's Newsletter and get a FREE book! kyliegilmore.com/newsletter

For text alerts on Kylie's new releases, text KYLIE to the number (888) 707-3025. (US only)

For more fun stuff check out Kylie's website https://www.kyliegilmore.com.

Thanks for reading *Almost Hitched*. I hope you enjoyed it. Would you like to know about new releases? You can sign up for my new release email list at kyliegilmore.com/newsletter. I promise not to clog your inbox! Only new release info, sales, and some fun giveaways.

I love to hear from readers! You can find me at:
kyliegilmore.com
Facebook.com/KylieGilmoreToo
Twitter @KylieGilmoreToo

If you liked Ian and Kate's story, please leave a review on your favorite retailer's website or Goodreads. Thank you.

9 781942 238218